This book is for you if.

- You are a parent looking to encourage and guide your child in the world of sports, at school, or simply in life.

- You are a teacher who wants to encourage reading of material which develops self-esteem, confidence, resilience, empathy, attitude and mindful mental health.

- You are a person who works with young children and wants to make an even greater positive impact on their lives.

- You are a child who is finding out about your strengths and weaknesses and want to build a mindset toolkit to deal with whatever life throws at you.

Take a look here to see Ross talk briefly about Katy.

http://bit.ly/KatyIntro

Dedication

Winifred A. McWilliam: Friend – Lord – Protector (Saxon Origin)
March 8th 1930 - May 23rd 2017

When my Mother eventually passed away from dementia in 2017, it was the end of an era – both my parents had gone. Being single, I felt alone, almost like an orphan. But I also felt compelled to honour her memory. Mum was always helping others, was actively involved in emotional health way before it became mainstream, and was simply an icon of her times. These qualities needed to be shared with a wider audience.

Katy Cupsworth is my attempt to 'do her proud' and create a lasting legacy that may well help young children…and their parents. I know that writing this book has certainly helped me reflect on her life, and, as a result of that process, I have reflected on my own life and where it will take me now. All I know at this moment in time, is that I have unfinished business as I honour Mum, as I honoured Dad & Danni in my CUPPA Series. This book is another key part of my journey.

"But somewhere in her life, I hope I made her proud."

The Amazing Journey of

KATY CUPSWORTH
THE PERFORMANCE WARRIOR

FINDING THE SIX SECRETS OF THE FOOTBALLING MINDSET

BY ROSS McWILLIAM

THE ULTIMATE GUIDE TO
SELF-DISCOVERY, POSITIVE MIND FITNESS
& IMPROVED PERFORMANCE

Published by
Filament Publishing Ltd
16, Croydon Road, Waddon, Croydon,
Surrey, CR0 4PA, United Kingdom
Telephone +44 (0)20 8688 2598
Fax +44 (0)20 7183 7186
info@filamentpublishing.com
www.filamentpublishing.com

ISBN 978-1-913192-48-8

Printed by 4edge Ltd

Contents

Mission 1 – Natural Belmont Born Lioness   19

Katy is a natural footballer and is focused on achieving her goal of becoming a professional footballer. Despite all her natural ability, she seems to lack something….and it's a 'stranger' whom she meets who helps her on her journey, although at first Katy is very wary of her. The journey starts and it's all fun and winning games. Then something happens, and the fun stops abruptly in the form of Meanie Marcie McGhee and the real mind games begin.

Mission 2 – The Cub Grows in Dutch Confidence   39

How will Katy fare against better players in a tournament in Holland? The answer lies in her response to being injured and the so called 'help' from Fred! Support from her parents and fellow players can take you so far, but to be successful you need something else. Has Katy got it when it really counts… taking a penalty to win a tournament?

Mission 3 – The Lioness is Bitten, but Will she Bite Back?   61

Katy learns from the past about Dick, Kerr's Ladies, and how they had to be resilient to withstand all the negativity about playing football. Katy has an opportunity to test her resilience against the Sanchez Sisters, but does she choose the right response, or does she react badly? Will this behaviour serve her well in the future on her journey to being a pro footballer?

Foreword

What the research tells is not far removed from our own informal observations – that there is no sure-fire recipe for success: outside of the laboratory, the human condition is beset with far too many variables for any one course of action to predict an outcome with anything close to 100% accuracy. In times past, for instance, it was thought that "Talent will out": given sufficient 'natural ability', success is assured. In more recent decades, the 'nurture' argument has often held sway – the claim that factors like effort, grit and persistence can guarantee success. In support of this, the nuanced and careful scholarship of people like Professor Carol Dweck has often been wildly over-simplified or reduced to formulaic exhortations to "Work harder" or "Believe in yourself and your dreams will come true". Neither extreme is true. The alchemy of success isn't exactly mysterious, but it is fearsomely complex. Ultimate success reflects the outworkings of a myriad of factors, of which natural ability can play an important part, but only in conjunction with opportunity, and a set of vital and largely non-cognitive factors which become especially crucial at times of crisis – when one's natural ability seems to be questioned or found unequal to the task.

In our pursuit of learning and ultimate achievement, the old saw teaches us that there's no substitute for experience. But the educator Neville West taught us something much more acute – that actually we don't learn from experience - we learn by reflecting on the experience. Experiences that facilitate self-reflection are therefore more likely to support learning than experiences which don't – however powerful that experience has been at the time. The author Ross McWilliam takes this insight to heart in his fictional account of a talented footballer striving to fulfil her dreams in the face of obstacles, doubts and challenges. Throughout the tale, packed as it is with incidents and opportunities, the young reader is invited to identify with the protagonist, Katy Cupsworth, and to engage actively in considering the choices she can – and should – make. It's therefore an active and multi-media read, encouraging reader agency and the chance to think about one's thinking. En route, there are many lessons to learn – not least the reality that talent alone is not enough. If it's true that there's no substitute for experience, there is a pretty decent second best: deep and personalised reflection on someone else's.

Dr Barry J Hymer
Emeritus Professor of Psychology in Education, University of Cumbria

Endorsement Quotes

"The arrival of Ross's tale of the challenges of Katy Cupsworth is a timely one. With the complexities of modern life, including social media, young people's mental health and well-being is under more pressure than ever before. It is crucially important therefore, that parents, teachers and all who are invested in supporting the growth and development of our young people, need to help with this.

It was the first sentence in M Scott Peck's book *The Road Less Travelled* which summed it up perfectly, 'life is difficult'. By developing the same tools and strategies that Katy uses to overcome the life challenges on her journey, I'm confident young people will be better equipped to cope and, indeed, thrive with the challenges that life will naturally bring."

Mark Burns FLPI
Leading Educational Speaker and Co-Author of Three Best-Selling Educational Books

"An effortless way to learn about a positive, resilient, and mentally healthy mindset whilst enjoying a journey full of adventures with Katy Cupsworth."

David Fann
Associate Headteacher, Former Secretary, National Association of Headteachers

"Over the years, I have been increasingly aware of the impact Ross has made in the learning and development of children and young adults. His latest book is an engaging story that also gives crucial strategies, toolkits and simple tips to enable children, parents and coaches to achieve 'mind fitness' in both football, and in life."

Mark Lawrenson
BBC Football Analyst, and Former Liverpool & Republic of Ireland Footballer

"I could really relate to the situations Katy faced in the book, and the choice sections in the book made me think about the power I have to make the best of the difficult situations that I might find myself in."

Gracie Burns
Aged 14, Blue Coat School, Liverpool

"This adventurous story about a football-loving girl also contains fun and educational missions and it teaches you, among other things, a positive way of thinking. Holland is also included in the story, very nice. Highly recommended, especially if you like sports!"

Sierra Meijn Santisima Trinidad
Aged 12, Jarige Scholier Uit Amsterdam, Holland

"Oh yes…I love this book. The last time when I was asked by my teacher to play piano in front of all my classmates, I felt so nervous and a little bit embarrassed. If I had read this book, I would have been more confident."

Jonathan
Aged 7, Primary School, London Borough of Bromley

"I really enjoyed this book. It was very funny but also filled with important life lessons. I would recommend it to anyone and cannot wait until the next book is released!"

Holly Foster
Aged 10, St Luke's C of E Primary, Formby

Introduction

I decided to write this book for two reasons. Firstly, to create a legacy for my Mother who passed away from dementia in 2017 after leading such a caring, nurturing and positive lifestyle. Secondly, in an age where there seems to be so much pressure and expectation on children, I wanted to offer a simple way of learning the skills that would enable children to not only survive this modern-day onslaught, but rather, could actually make them thrive in this environment. I always believe that whenever there is a threat, there is almost always an opportunity and I see this book as such an opportunity for children, parents and teachers.

The book is written around a partly fictional story, but with factual content relevant to developing a positive mindset. Rather than state facts and tell the reader they must do X,Y,Z, the book revolves around a journey where the reader has choices to make and consequences to experience. Reading is easy, and often funny, and learning is sometimes subtle (implicit), and sometimes very obvious (explicit), as in the embedded QR code videos of Fred Fixes and global mindset examples. There is an opportunity to measure your progress by taking the SCREAM test at the start, and then again at the end of the book. In addition, there are a number of free downloads which can be accessed which will help with consolidating learning. Finally, there are a number of questions and key words at the end of each Mission which may be useful to embed learning (the key word definitions are at the end of the book).

Over my many years of working with children, and young adults, I have found that when you tell someone to do something in a didactic, disciplinary manner, they may not do it, even if it's good for them! If children sometimes don't know they are learning, and are enjoying the book, then this surely is the way to go. At the end of this book, the reader, be it children, parents, teachers or those people involved in the precious education of our next generation, will possess a highly effective and practical toolkit of skills which they can call upon in good times, and in times of challenge. This is an aid to development and many children will benefit from these.

However, sadly, some children may have experienced a level of trauma which makes accessing consistent change more difficult. In these cases, having worked over the years with this specific type of challenge, it may be more suitable to use the book and resources in conjunction with a trained professional such as an educational psychologist or child psychiatrist. Nevertheless, armed with this knowledge and toolkit, along with their life experiences, it is only a matter time before success for many children is achieved. It is inevitable, believe me.

Ross

About Ross

Since the death of his Father, and Danni, his beautiful young niece, Ross felt compelled to create a legacy to honour them. He did this by creating the CUPPA Book Series which helps young children develop a confident mindset. Following the loss of his Mother in 2017, Ross was determined to create another legacy, and this was to be Katy Cupsworth.

No matter what happens in life, Ross is a firm believer that every experience can ultimately help you grow and improve as a person, as long as you have belief. In Ross's own words, "it's not who gets there first that counts, just as long as you get there!" This echoes Ross's struggles in life and his continual quest to improve himself and reach his full potential.

Ross has been involved in educating children, young adults and senior professionals for over 30 years, has visited over 1,000 schools, colleges and universities, and has probably changed the lives of one million people. In this time, Ross has developed not only his knowledge, but crucially, the way he tries to understand, engage and empower his audiences.

Beyond this acquired professionalism, Ross has felt the real sadness of his own academic, health and life challenges. This has been borne out with him failing all his qualifications at school, going through acne face and body scarring, incurring disability and experiencing the devastating deaths of both his parents. It was a result of this devastation, of losing his 'life mentors,' that he decided to create a legacy to honour them both.

This started in 2017, when he released the CUPPA Book Series. This legacy of helping children reach their full potential in life, has been further bolstered now in 2019, with the release of Katy Cupsworth. Belief in oneself, and reaching for your potential in life is a precious gift that Ross's parents gave to him, but which wasn't fully appreciated by Ross until they had left him.

"I was standing on the shoulders of giants, but never realised it."
Ross A McWilliam

Conclusion – If you only get one thing from this book, I hope that one thing is a belief that you can and will improve on your own journey. On reflection, your parents and other mentors, are crucial to instilling this belief, whether you know that or not. So, surround yourself with people who are 100% behind you. Life, as I have found out, can be brilliant, but when it's not, there are always lessons to be learned… you just need to find them.

This book and its resources may prove helpful to you and your parents and other mentors, so try and be patient. Not all your lessons come at once, and when we reflect, it is often then that crucial things can be learned.

If you liked Katy Cupsworth, maybe you might like to join CUPPA (www.cuppajourney.com) on his amazing journey? Or maybe you want to wait until I have written my third book, The Amazing Journey of *Alex, Roxy & Tiger*, which is a journey into the world of hidden 'special' knowledge and achievements.

Acknowledgements

Wilbur Smith said when you write, tell a story about things that you know, things that are fact or based in fact. Being one of the most published authors on the planet, I took his advice and built my storylines around my own family. Therefore, I must thank the McWilliam family for providing the inspiration for both Katy and CUPPA. Central to this inspiration were my parents, Bob and Wyn. They gave me an inbuilt unshakeable belief that I could achieve something in life. I hope they are as proud of me, as I was of them.

Secondly, the constant rejections from publishers only served to spur me on, so thank you. Not being rich, famous or connected, my motivations kept soaring on the back of each rejection….until Chris Day at Filament Publishing saw something in me, in my storylines and saw how relevant these messages were in today's world of young people and their challenges.

Teachers Mark Noblet and David Fann helped steer me between the mid-line of education and entertainment. It's no good just preaching to children, but it's also not a case of trying to be funny – there must be a seamless blend of education and entertainment. I call this 'edutainment' and I hope the readers see this.

Finally, thank you to Matt Sullivan who created the unique black and white illustrations of Katy Cupsworth and Colour Cover Ilustrator David Robinson. Good illustrations bring the story to life and allows the reader to 'get into the story' and Matt and David achieved this expertly.

Scream 48

Why not measure your **SCREAM 48** score BEFORE you start reading? Then, when you have finished the book, why not measure again and compare your scores?
Answer each question with only one answer. Add up your scores after 12 questions to find your **SCREAM 48**.

1   You value yourself highly in terms of your own achievements and qualities
Strongly Agree – Agree – Disagree – Strongly Disagree

2   You doubt your self-worth in terms of your own abilities
Strongly Agree – Agree – Disagree – Strongly Disagree

3   You are rarely scared of life's day to day challenges
Strongly Agree – Agree – Disagree – Strongly Disagree

4   If you feel nervous, these feelings can often stop you attempting challenges
Strongly Agree – Agree – Disagree – Strongly Disagree

5   You can often give up completing challenges
Strongly Agree – Agree – Disagree – Strongly Disagree

6   You recognise the need to re-charge and review your strengths if you can't complete a challenge
Strongly Agree – Agree – Disagree – Strongly Disagree

7   More often than not, you consider the needs of others
Strongly Agree – Agree – Disagree – Strongly Disagree

8   You will agree to a group decision even if you feel you're in the right
Strongly Agree – Agree – Disagree – Strongly Disagree

9   You feel you have certain strengths and certain weaknesses
    Strongly Agree – Agree – Disagree – Strongly Disagree

10 You think over time you can't improve your strengths and can't reduce
    your weaknesses
    Strongly Agree – Agree – Disagree – Strongly Disagree

11 You are calm in a stressful situation
    Strongly Agree – Agree – Disagree – Strongly Disagree

12 You don't have a range of skills and strategies which allow you to
    overcome nerves
    Strongly Agree – Agree – Disagree – Strongly Disagree

Scores:

	Strongly Agree	Agree	Disagree	Strongly Disagree
1	4	3	2	1
2	1	2	3	4
3	4	3	2	1
4	1	2	3	4
5	1	2	3	4
6	4	3	2	1
7	4	3	2	1
8	4	3	2	1
9	4	3	2	1
10	1	2	3	4
11	4	3	2	1
12	1	2	3	4

Results:

1-12   You are at the beginning of your journey. With good support and your sustained efforts, you may well make progress and go far on your journey to a better you.

13-24   You have made some progress, but you need to keep going. Learn from your mistakes and be prepared to keep pushing yourself and your journey may well surprise you

25-36   You have made good progress and there is more to come if you continue to learn and apply yourself

37-48   You have made excellent progress, but you can get complacent. You must keep learning, help others, and see the value in your journey.

Mission 1

NATURAL BELMONT
BORN LIONESS

Katy is great at football,
But what if she takes a fall,
Can she get back on her feet?
Or will she fail and taste defeat?

"Shoot Katy…. let them have it!" shouted an excitable Ted, the team manager from the touchline. Katy wanted to shoot, but was almost put off by the shout from Ted, who was very annoying at times, mainly because he also happened to be her dad.

Katy was waiting just a second until the ball bobbled up. As soon as it did, her left foot connected with it. Moments later, all that could be heard was the whoosh of the ball hitting the net as it ripped out the ground pegs holding it in place. The helpless goalie and her team were the latest victims of the 'Screamer.'

You see, that was Katy Cupsworth's strength. She knew, even at a young age, that she had a natural talent for football. She had practised with a ball on her own since she was six years old and had instantly taken to the sport. Katy was also quite tall for her age and had long thin legs that she used to generate power in her shots, and speed around the pitch. Maybe because there were no leagues around at that time for girls, she had become frustrated and so had focused on proving that girls were just as good as boys, and maybe even better.

She would often beat boys at 'keepie uppie' ball juggling and teased them relentlessly as they struggled to get the ball off her when she was doing her fast, mazy dribbles. This frustration though turned out to be a good thing, as she developed the 'Screamer' shot – her secret weapon that no boy could ever match! Her cousin Chris 'Cuppa' Cupsworth had found this out to his cost. Chris was often in the firing line as a reluctant goalkeeper in the back garden. He regularly collected various injuries trying to stop her ferocious 'Screamer.' Once he was hit so hard in a sensitive area that he had a voice like Mickey Mouse for a week.

"That's my girl" said Ted proudly. He then started to mumble to himself about what a player Katy was and then randomly shouted out "she's the next Marta you know" to anyone who was listening. You could say Ted was very proud of his footballing daughter. He was so proud; he even made her Captain.

"Ted, now, don't go getting too excited and putting pressure on Katy," warned Felicity, Ted's anxious ex-wife. "Marta is a world-famous Brazilian footballer; she's spent years crafting her skills. Katy's still young, and we haven't won the match yet, and there are still ten minutes to go."

The minutes ticked by slowly, and with the score at 1-0 to Belmont Avenue, Katy picked up the ball in midfield, played a 'one two ' with Ranvir, the Belmont centre half, before dribbling it to the corner flag to waste time. Her opponents tried to get the ball off her, but her combination of dribbles and ball juggling made that task almost impossible. The frustration of her opponents ended when a loud whistle shrilled. The referee had blown her whistle for full time.

"Well done Belmont. Another victory. We will have this league wrapped up by Christmas, but for now let's focus on the present …'wrapped'…'Christmas'…'present'…get it?" said Ted laughing at his own jokes as all adults do.

Felicity also liked to win, but she also liked fair play and had quietly instilled in all the players the value of sportsmanship before and after matches. Felicity was like a mother hen, looking after the needs of the young girls. These needs could be first aid, preparing half time refreshments, post-match buffets and even putting an arm around anyone who needed a hug and a few kind words of support. It was like she was physio, coach and assistant manager all rolled into one.

Ted too, wore many football hats. Apart from manager, and bad joke teller, he was also club secretary organising fixtures with the league committee, head groundsman responsible for cutting the grass, and operations manager, which meant he put up the nets and corner flags on match days!

As the Belmont players shook hands with their vanquished opponents, Ted and Felicity smiled at each other. They made an impressive football management team when they weren't arguing about what was best for Katy.

This impressive management team had gone through some difficult times that had sadly led to the break-up of their marriage, and subsequent divorce. Strangely, it all started when Katy took an interest in football, and then started to show a natural ability for it. Ted recognised this natural ability and was keen to teach her new skills almost every day in the back garden after school. If that wasn't enough, he took her to live football matches to watch the best players, and when they couldn't do that, they watched it live on TV. Ted pushed her into the footballing spotlight at every opportunity, as he was convinced she would make a professional in the Women's Premier Football League (WPFL). Football was taking over Katy's life, which Katy quite liked, but it had affected her progress in school.

Felicity though, preferred a more measured and protected development of Katy's talent so she could develop in her own time, without added pressure and expectation. Whether she would become a professional footballer or not, Felicity just wanted her to be happy and always try her best at whatever she did in life.

They used to argue about who was doing the washing up and drying, whilst at other times it would be about Ted's snoring which kept Felicity, and even the neighbours, awake at nights. But most of all, they argued about Katy. This is what led to their divorce and now they lived apart with Katy staying at Felicity's during the week, and at Ted's every weekend. The 'school v football' debate was still the continual cause of many arguments. Ted and Felicity didn't know it, but Katy had nicknames for both of them. Their rivalry sometimes spilled over onto match days and had prompted Katy to call them UniTed and FeliCity. It was like having a Manchester derby every week!

However, for all their disagreements in the past, both Ted and Felicity were now trying to be nicer to each other for the sake of Katy, and Katy liked this, as she liked being the centre of attention.

As a result of the new living arrangements though, Katy didn't have as much time to see her Grandma Wyn. Katy had always been very close to her and liked the way she was always calm and supportive, but never in a way that threatened her mum Felicity. As a child, Wyn was known as Winifred, and was educated at Winckley Square Convent where she showed impressive academic ability. Following school, she worked in the important role of company secretary at the local Courtaulds factory which made fabrics and chemicals.

But this career path was to end when she met Grandad Bob, and together they embarked on creating a loving family of four children, which many years later, yielded four grandchildren. Sadly, tragedy was to strike in the years to come, as their grand-daughter Danni, Katy's cousin, passed away when she was only 21.

In their prime, both Wyn and Bob were pioneers in healthy living and were always trying out new ways to keep healthy, either in body or in mind. They had once owned and operated a health gymnasium, The Apollo. Grandad Bob would take the weight and fitness classes, while Grandma Wyn delivered Yoga and Buddhist meditation classes. Wyn had a yearning to travel and visited many places all over the world, sometimes with Bob, and then on her own after Grandad Bob died. She called these trips her learning journeys as she sought to improve her understanding of life, and her favourite place of learning was Tibet in the Far East.

Above all, Wyn would help anyone who needed it, family, friends or complete strangers. That was who she was and why Katy loved her so much. Katy adored her attitude to life, her ability to never give in, and her sense of teamwork. She had modelled herself on Grandma Wyn and had embraced her qualities. But Katy being Katy, was a little inconsistent, and sometimes ended up being frustrated, sometimes even looking for short cuts. This was something Grandma Wyn never did.

As the season unfolded, Belmont Avenue were seemingly unstoppable. In October, they were top of the league by six points and there was a real buzz and expectation about what this team could achieve.

"Do you know what Katy?" asked Ted looking at Katy, not waiting for her to reply, "if we keep playing like this, we could win the treble this season by winning the League, Cup and the new Invitational Trophy, and maybe even Ivor Contract, the famous scout, will sign you up?"

"What's the Invitational Trophy dad?" asked Katy curiously.

"The IT, as it has become known, is a weekend tournament played just after Christmas between four teams, one each from Scotland, Holland, Belgium and England. To qualify as one of the four teams, your team has to not only demonstrate many aspects of fair play, but must not have had any red cards in the season up until Christmas."

"No 'cards' at Christmas dad, that seems a bit unfair, like Scrooge…that's not in the giving spirit for the 'season'?" said Katy cheekily.

"Listen Katy, I tell the jokes around here!" said Ted smiling at her as he continued to explain about the IT.

"Whichever country wins the IT can host it the following year. This year the tournament is being held in Delft, Holland. The IT is something that both players and parents want to win as it would be a nice trip during the festive period," explained Ted.

"Will I miss lessons?" asked Katy enthusiastically, becoming more interested about the possibility of missing school.

"Good try Katy, but it's during the school holidays!"

Katy was feeling good about her football and everything was going so well in her life, except for one small thing…. school! Katy didn't like it. It wasn't that she hated it, far from it. It was just that if she couldn't be the best, she would quickly lose interest, especially when challenged. This was her **fear of failure**. This was really evident when she had to concentrate hard in tests. She felt she wasn't naturally clever if she didn't 'get it' first time and was almost looking for an excuse to give up when she came across any difficulty. This fear of failure reared its ugly head at the first sign of a problem. Even in PE, she would try her best, but if others seemed to be doing better than her, she would become argumentative, even hot tempered and would often just give up. This poor habit was not helping her develop.

But with football it was different. She was the best and everything came to her naturally. Her passion for being the best kept driving her on to keep practising, trying new moves on the pitch and believing that one day she would be a professional footballer. However, this positive attitude to football had recently been challenged, and she was starting to use her poor school habits as an excuse if things didn't go her way on the football pitch.

Trying to keep her grounded and on the straight and narrow was Ted, and he was her greatest **role model**. Another role model in her family was her cousin Chris who would often pop round to see Katy.

'Ding-dong' sounded the doorbell.

"Katy can you get the door please" shouted Ted from the top of the stairs.

Katy opened the door and Chris was stood there, a football under one arm and his finished homework in the other, which Katy usually copied.

As Chris walked through the door, Katy grabbed the homework and started to copy it.

"Hey Chris, don't you find school boring, especially doing all our homework?" asked Katy as she scribbled furiously, taking advantage of Chris's hard work. Chris didn't like helping Katy in this way, but felt under pressure from her. This certainly wasn't a quality that Grandma Wyn would have been proud of.

"Not really Katy" sighed Chris. "At first, I struggled, as I didn't believe I was as good as everyone else. But after my amazing journey around the world I found some belief in myself, and I started to give things a go at school. Through looking at things differently, I became more confident and resilient, and learned to appreciate my unique qualities and achievements."

"Your amazing journey?" asked Katy.

"Yes, I went to London first, then Moscow, then Toronto, then Machu Picchu, then Islamabad. I met some weird people such as Mrs Hardcastle, Mr Just Do it, Pete Positivity and even came across a guy called Willie Fail who tried to make me doubt myself. At one point, I met Mixed Grylls, the intrepid explorer and he invited me onto the show 'I'm Not A Celebrity Get Me In Here' – I had to do a bush-tucker trial! At the end everyone called me Cuppa as I developed a real belief in myself. I even met Grandad Bob again, but he was called Alf!"

"You and your imagination Chris" sighed Katy, thinking her cousin was just a day dreamer. However, a small part of her had noticed a positive change in Chris recently. He seemed happier. He was doing better at school. He was more cheerful and positive. Maybe he had been on some kind of journey, or maybe he was just growing up.

"Believe it or not Katy, I am different, better now. You never know, you might even have your own amazing journey one day!" said Chris smiling to himself, as if he knew something Katy didn't.

"Anyway, it's getting late and I better be off. I need to start my next homework, so you can copy that as well" said Chris sarcastically. "It's school tomorrow and I love it. You really should do your own homework if you want to get ahead in life," he exclaimed as he ran out of the door and down the road back to his own house.

Once the homework had been fully copied and instantly forgotten, Katy watched her favourite TV Show 'Short Cuts For Winners With No Effort' and then went to bed, not giving Chris's 'amazing journey' a second thought. All she could think about was Belmont Avenue's next match on Saturday - the first-round cup match against Frenchwood Park.

Saturday came around quickly, and it was quite windy as Ted struggled to put up the nets. Even the corner flag posts were swaying in the breeze. At one point, Ted and Felicity wondered if the match would go ahead. But as kick off approached, the wind softened, and the sun came out, making it possible for the important cup match to go ahead.

Their opponents, Frenchwood Park, were well known in girls' football. The team itself was not the most skilful, but they had a reputation for being aggressive, with a win at all costs approach. In their captain, Meanie Marcie McGhee, they possessed the biggest, and scariest player ever to play girls' football. She was nearly 6ft tall, hands and feet as big as a man's and a tackle that could take out both a player and a spectator at the same time. Her nickname was M3 and that was also the name of the local accident and emergency hospital ward! For M3, the rules were meant to be broken, like bones, win or lose, and that mentality went for anyone who dared to stand in her way.

Frenchwood Park had a large following of supporters who loved it when they beat the opposition – 'beat' being the important word. Many didn't mind if they lost, as long as they got to hurt the opposition!

Most of the Belmont players were more than a little nervous and wanted to keep their limbs attached to their bodies, all except Katy Cupsworth. She loved a football challenge as it was a chance to show what she could do on the pitch and she believed in herself and her abilities. M3 and their supporters weren't going to scare her.

Within two minutes of kick off, Meanie Marcie McGhee had elbowed 'Roly' Paula, the Belmont keeper, and had also 'accidently' run into the ref who subsequently tumbled over temporarily losing his whistle in the mud. It was her way of saying she was in charge.

"Throw it to Katy" shouted Ted as 'Roly' Paula held the ball. 'Roly' was almost as big as M3, but didn't use her size in an unfair way. She wasn't the best keeper in the league, and didn't even look like a keeper, but she had a strong positive body image of herself. She also had great self-belief and never dwelled on mistakes. She just always valued herself, in terms of her abilities, did her best, and kept learning from her mistakes.

'Roly' Paula threw the ball out to Tick Tock Tracey, the tiny Belmont winger. Tick Tock wasn't the fastest or most skilful player on the pitch, but she always seemed to be in the right place at the right time, and this was her skill, hence her adopted nickname. She had turned a weakness into a strength, which was something Katy had difficulty doing.

Tick Tock then played it to Katy on the wing. Quickly, Katy pushed it through the legs of the wing back and raced beyond her towards Frenchwood's goal. Along the touchline, she could hear the chants of the Frenchwood supporters…"Meanie Marcie McGhee… kill, kill, kill!"

The crowd knew that waiting for Katy was M3.

Then a lone voice from the crowd called out, "She's pathetic and skinny, and only plays because her dad's the manager!" The rest of the crowd picked up on this and started calling out "Daddy long legs' girl."

M3 joined in by goading her, "Come to mummy…. you're not good enough…. you're in with the big girls now," as she stared menacingly at Katy.

The wind started to blow again as Katy pushed the ball up to M3 and tried to tease her with her step overs. But then she noticed a strange look in the eyes of M3. It was as if M3 wasn't even interested in the ball, she just had eyes for Katy. For the first time in her footballing life, Katy felt nervous. The crowd and M3 had got into her head.

Katy tried to flick the ball up and over the head of M3. But her body just froze and she mis-kicked the ball out of play. To add injury to insult, Katy slipped and M3 used the opportunity to 'accidentally' sit on Katy's head with a big thud. Katy ended up dazed in a heap on the muddy pitch. M3 and the Frenchwood supporters started to laugh louder and louder.

To add to her embarrassment, a gust of wind at that moment blew a huge pair of pink granny-type knickers off a neighbour's washing line. They hit Katy full in the face and now the entire crowd started to laugh at her.

The wind was gusting more strongly, and Katy was wondering why nobody was looking after her, or why her team-mates had not consoled her. It even crossed her mind why M3 hadn't stepped on her with her size 10 boots. It was if the whole game was at a standstill, as if time itself had stopped still. All that could be heard was the whistle of the wind, until a weird voice interrupted her thoughts.

"Katy darling isn't it a little muddy to be sitting down?" asked a lone gentle voice.

Katy couldn't see who was talking to her, but as she looked up, she did notice the voice was coming from a little cloud all on its own.

"Who cares?" snapped Katy defiantly, pulling the huge pink knickers off her face and looking round for the owner of the voice. "Where are you? Why can't I see you?"

"I care, Katy," said the soft voice. "So do your teammates. And so, I suspect, do you, deep down. As for seeing me, well, you'll just have to be patient. All in good time."

Katy shook her head, and was now feeling a little bit worried that she might be concussed. She looked up to the sky and saw the lone cloud again. "Are you real?" she said out loud. "Who are you?"

"I'm Fred," came the voice. "I'm your friend and you're the only one who can hear me, and in time you will be able to see me properly. I'm here to help you."

"Well Fred, you had better get off my case as I have a footy match to win," said Katy impatiently.

"That's fine for now, but I need my knickers back first Katy!" said Fred laughing.

Katy spoke up angrily, "OK, have your Bridget Jones' knickers!"

Fred continued to talk to her.

"Katy Cupsworth, you have some belief in yourself. That is clear for anyone to see. Some people call this **self-esteem** – I call it your belief in yourself. To do anything in life, including being a pro footballer, you must believe in yourself. For example, a house needs a strong foundation so that it can be built to support itself and protect itself from bad weather, including floating knickers ..." said Fred, almost laughing again.

"But to really develop this belief, you also need to believe in your own **physical self-worth**. Be positive about your physical self and don't let yourself, or anyone else, put you down purely because your appearance may be different to others.

"Now, you Katy are tall, and may I say it, a little wiry, but you must embrace your appearance. Some people may see your appearance, be it your face or your body, as an opportunity to put you down. That is their problem, not yours. You must overcome this by rising above any negative comments and show people what you are made of, both on and off the pitch… and your funny long legs may well prove to be your secret weapon on the pitch. Eventually, you may start to accept, and value your physical self, and maybe eventually, you could celebrate it?

"For example, do you think 'Roly' Paula thinks less of herself as she is bigger than most other girls of her age? She has physical self-worth and never lets anyone put her down. She models herself on goalies such as our own Rachel Finnis-Brown, the ex-Everton and England goalkeeper, Hope Solo from the USA and Nadine Angerer from Germany. They are the foundation of a team. They never let anyone, or anything shake their physical self-worth," said Fred, finally finishing off the lecture.

"But your belief in yourself and physical self-worth will not just happen overnight. It could be a life-time process where you nurture and cherish both. Or look at it another way. Imagine you are at school sitting in an English class."

Katy started to scowl as she remembered how much she didn't like anything to do with school.

"So, self-worth is a verb. You remember, a doing word. That means you must do it all the time. If you do this, then this results in confidence, which is the noun, meaning not being scared," pronounced Fred.

"What's confidence Fred?" asked Katy feeling a little confused.

"I can't tell you everything at once Katy. Well, actually I can, but you will just have to wait until I can show you a good example," replied Fred, as if knowing what was going to happen in the future.

Katy was getting more confused, and when she was confused, she would often get angry.

"Listen Fred, you know nothing about me. So, don't give me your advice. I'm Katy Cupsworth the footballer you know!" replied an angry Katy.

Fred didn't let Katy's angry interruption stop the lecture.

"I know personally, that you have got this by belief in yourself from your parents, by making great friends and team-mates, by practising and developing your football skills, by seeing your own progress, by scoring goals, by being made captain. This is just a test. Never doubt yourself or you are letting Doubting Debbie into your life," said Fred.

"Doubting Debbie?" said Katy looking even more puzzled.

"Yes, she represents all your doubts and if you let her into your head, she can even make you doubt your own name! But once she's in, she's a real pain. You must have met her at school as you're always doubting yourself there, unlike your cousin Chris," said the now slightly serious Fred.

"Give me a break. Doubting Debbie, what sort of name is that? How do you know my parents and Chris?" pleaded Katy looking for answers to her questions.

The wind was whistling even more loudly now, as Katy waited for the reply from Fred.

"Forget about me," said Fred, "this is all about you and your choices. Are you going to react negatively or respond positively and believe in yourself? What *type* of person are you?

Here are your choices….and consequences:"

Katy has three **choices**:

1   Get up and get on with the game, even though she doesn't think she can beat M3.
2   Be brave and trust her skills and believe she can beat M3 next time.
3   Pretend to be injured and get her dad to carry her off the pitch .

Which choice should Katy make?

Here are the **consequences**:

1   Katy continues to doubt herself, and Doubting Debbie becomes her new BFF.
2   People respect and admire Katy, and see what makes her a good leader.
3   People see Katy wasn't really injured and think she's a quitter. They lose trust in her.

Katy wondered what to do. She could get up and get on with the game, but was she strong enough to beat M3? Or she could trust her superior footballing skills to get past her, and win for her team. Or maybe she should just say she was injured, and get her dad to take her off the pitch and out of the situation altogether?

Katy picked **Choice 1**. She had to finish the game. She got back on her feet, looking nervously at M3. It was time to play football.

But would that choice come back to haunt her the next time she faced M3, and maybe later down the road on her journey to becoming a pro footballer?

The wind and Fred had gone as quickly as they had come.

As the match continued, Belmont had most of the possession, yet it was Frenchwood who had the clearer chances. 'Roly' Paula and her defence stood firm and kept a clean sheet. Half time came and went quickly.

Two minutes into the second half, Frenchwood were awarded a free kick just outside the Belmont penalty area. This was just the invitation needed for the star players of Frenchwood – the Sanchez Sisters.

Sarina and Sadia Sanchez were subtle in their ways. The sisters were very skilful and competitive, especially at set pieces. But sometimes they let their competitiveness get the better of them and wouldn't think twice about tripping an opponent, or worse still, misplacing an elbow in the face of anyone who dared to go past them with the ball.

While M3 was the obvious physical threat to the opposition, the Sanchez Sisters presented a more subtle, sneakier physical threat.

Sarina Sanchez grabbed the ball and placed it next to the referee. As the referee marched the wall back ten metres, Sadia subtly moved it to create a better angle for the free kick. The Frenchwood keeper came up to add her height and weight in the box.

On the whistle, Sarina chipped the ball to Sadia who volleyed it towards the goal. It flew like a rocket straight towards 'Roly' Paula. Something had to give. Either Paula would somehow stop the shot, or it would take her into the back of the net and win the cup game for Frenchwood.

The ball was flying like a missile towards Paula, but she stood her ground. She had belief in herself and wasn't going to let a little temporary pain stop her doing her best.

The next noise that could be heard was a collision of plastic on face, as the ball moulded into the contours of Paula's face. Paula was instantly pushed backwards, and both the ball and her face, which was stuck to it, were moving closer and closer to the goal line.

"'Roly'.... stop!" shouted Ted.

"Paula, you can do it" screamed Felicity who was almost as anxious as Ted.

Paula, though, had it all under control. Her strong legs quickly halted her backwards steps and the ball dropped to the floor. She picked it up.

With the ball now in her hands, Paula kicked it downfield to 'Ambling' Andrea, the slow-motion Belmont midfielder, who always took her time on the ball. Her slowness allowed her to lay a perfectly timed pass into the path of Katy. Katy then raced onto the ball and quickly gained possession as virtually all the Frenchwood team were left hopelessly in her wake. All the Frenchwood team that was, apart from M3.

Katy dribbled the ball up to M3, trembling as she did so. All Katy could think of was personal survival, and so she dribbled away from M3 and avoided a possible injury. But her wayward dribble took her too far away from the goals, and she ran the ball over the dead ball line for a goal kick. But there was no time for the goal kick. The full-time whistle blew, and the match ended in a disappointing draw.

A gentle breeze blew Katy's fringe into her eyes and as she re-arranged her hair, and the lone cloud came into view again.

"Young Katy, you scraped through today, by avoiding M3, but at the expense of not winning the game. You have demonstrated some belief in yourself by practising, learning from situations and sometimes believing you are more than good enough. This is the first secret of the footballing mindset.

"But you need to demonstrate this when it really counts in the big matches. This is footballing confidence, which is all about performance without being scared, even of people like M3, or even the Sanchez Sisters. When you start to enjoy the pressure situations, without being scared of anyone, I will show you my **Fred Fix**. In other words, my own way of solving a problem."

Before Katy could ask what a Fred Fix was, Fred had interrupted her.

"But more of this when you travel to Delft to meet the mighty Delft Dynamoes, Edinburgh Eagles and Bruges Braves!"

Daft, brave eagles and a Fred Fix. What planet is this Fred voice on, thought Katy.

Mission 1 Questions

- What was Katy's dream?
- What was Katy's secret weapon?
- How had the 'Screamer' been developed?
- Why did Katy's mum and dad divorce?
- Why was Katy so fond of her Grandma?
- What is the "IT"?
- What was the purpose of Cuppa's amazing journey?
- Describe how you feel about Katy copying Cuppa's homework.
- Who do you think Fred is?
- Who or what is Doubting Debbie?
- What did Katy learn about self-esteem?

Key Words

Fear of Failure

Role Model

Self-Esteem

Physical Self-Worth

Fred Fix

Global Video links

http://bit.ly/KatyCupA

http://bit.ly/KatyCupB

http://bit.ly/KatyCupC

Mission 2

THE CUB GROWS IN DUTCH CONFIDENCE

An overseas football tournament in the Netherlands,
Does Katy take it with both hands?
A chance to be No 1,
Or is it an opportunity gone?

t was November, and not only were Belmont Avenue winning each and every match, but Katy was coming on leaps and bounds. She was the top scorer in the League with 21 goals after only 12 games. Her 'Screamer' left foot shot was the talk of all the opposition players and managers. Whenever any team played Belmont Avenue, all that was mentioned was how to stop Katy scoring. They would mark her tight and even put two players on her. But this did not stop Katy. She would use her speed, generated by her long, gangly legs, to elude the markers in the box, and would often 'let rip' outside the box even before her markers had approached her! Her confidence was growing, along with the effectiveness of the 'Screamer'.

As Christmas approached, Ted was almost certain they'd be playing in the IT. They had a ten-point lead in the league. They were also at the top of the Fair Play League, with zero red cards to their name. But he knew that just one could be enough to end their dream of competing in Holland. Felicity was helping the cause, constantly instilling sportsmanship in all the players, and that impressed the Fair Play League officials. There was one more game to play, against Strangeways United, before Ted could be completely sure they'd be making that trip.

The final game before the Christmas break was held at the home of Anchor Inn WFC. Within 10 minutes of kick off, Katy had scored two more goals to add to her growing tally. One was the usual bullet 'Screamer', and the other a shot from Ranvir, that deflected off her backside. This was a really 'cheeky' goal, but Katy didn't mind how she scored.

However, as the match progressed there was an increased nervousness coming from both Ted and Felicity, and the rest of the parents as they were getting closer to a trip to Holland. This nervousness was now being felt by all the Belmont players as the girls started to worry about the possibility of getting a red card. Their confidence was being taken apart. Players started backing out of challenges, and this led to more possession being given to Anchor Inn WFC.

With less than 2 minutes left to play, Anchor Inn WFC midfield player Sammi Samurai intercepted a pass in midfield. Sammi was easily the quickest player on the pitch, and could cut up a defence with one dribble, like a knife going through butter. Hence Sammi's nickname BK - Butter Knife.

She easily 'sliced' passed Ambling Andrea, the slow Belmont midfielder, before 'spreading' the ball wide and collecting it herself. She then found herself bearing down on the penalty spot. Sammi then slid the ball past 'Roly' Paula, who accidentally made contact with Sammi. The ball rolled into the back of the net to the 'utterly butterly' dismay of the whole Belmont team and supporters. The Anchor Inn WFC fans were chanting out two words, 'Butter Knife…Butter Knife.'

The ref turned to face 'Roly' Paula. Everyone on the Belmont team held their breath as he reached for his pocket. Was he going to treat Paula's contact as an off-the-ball offence, and punish her with a yellow card? If he thought it was deliberate, he would give a red card, and the IT trip would be over even before it had begun. All the Belmont players waited anxiously. Time seemed to stand still. The ref pulled out a card and showed it to Paula.

"Thank goodness…it's only yellow" shouted a relieved Ted.

"Forget the yellow….it's orange all the way now, as we're off to Holland!" replied Felicity.

Christmas Day was only a week away and it came and went quickly that year, probably because everyone connected with Belmont Avenue was eagerly counting the days down until the day they would travel to Holland to compete in the IT.

At 6am on December 29th, Ted drove the 17-seater minibus to Belmont Recreation

Ground to pick up the players, plus a few parents who had volunteered to help out on the minibus journey. The rest of the parents took their own cars, and as they all left the 'Rec', Ted sounded his horn and all the parents followed his lead. Felicity had fixed a banner to the side of the minibus that read "Belmont Avenue on Tour – Win, Lose or Draw - Play Fair to All." Some parents had red and white English flags which were attached to their cars. It was an impressive convoy of vehicles that took to the road down south to Harwich in Essex where the ferry would take them to Hook of Holland.

The day also held a special sad significance for Ted and Felicity. It would have been their fifteenth wedding anniversary that day.

The ferry ride across was a little choppy which made the parents worry, but all the girls loved it. Although this was the first time many of the girls had been away from home, an adventure beckoned, and a little bumpy ferry ride wasn't going to dampen their spirits. Well, almost all the girls loved it. Ambling Andrea, who as usual, was slow to be sick, but once she started, she couldn't stop. This resulted in a recently consumed fried egg breakfast being deposited on Felicity's special £100 trip haircut. Felicity was not amused. Ted was quick to respond, "It's not an 'egg-cellent' haircut now is it Felicity?......But I bet you girls are all 'egg-cited' to be playing overseas soon?" said Ted laughing at his own jokes again.

Felicity was still not amused, but decided to join in the fun. "Any more of that Ted and your 'eggs-wife' will be very upset. Now the 'yolk' is on you!"

"You poor 'chick'" said Ted as he continued to 'crack' more jokes.

Felicity moaned her disapproval at Ted's so-called jokes and admitted defeat. She was 'beaten' like a whisked egg!

They touched down at Hook of Holland and from there it was only a 35-minute road trip to Delft. Felicity gave Ted a break from driving, as they now liked to take turns to help each other out. The only downside to this for Ted was that Felicity got all the girls singing at the top of their voices and that effectively stopped Ted having a cheeky nap at the back of the bus. However, Felicity knew this was a great way to improve team spirit and made the girls sing as loud as they could, much to the annoyance of Ted.

The first sight of Holland that stuck with Katy were the windmills, so many of them turning slowly in the wind. Everywhere they went they would always see a windmill. It was so different to what she had experienced before, but it was also strangely reassuring, but she didn't know why.

Felicity, with her new hairstyle and unique aroma, parked up the minibus at the Delft Arena. There was little time to change as their first match was about to start in under an hour. The tight travel schedule dictated this lack of preparation, and this was something that all the girls had to deal with.

Crowds of excited parents and young girls started to gather as the IT was about to start. A tall man with a microphone approached the main stand and stood up in front of the crowd from the Directors' Box.

"Ladies and gentlemen, players and officials…welcome to the IT. This year we have four teams competing to lift the prestigious trophy. Here are your teams.

Please welcome from Scotland, Edinburgh Eagles, captained by Tania Swift.

Please welcome from Belgium, Bruges Braves, captained by Evie Hazard.

Please welcome from England, Belmont Avenue, captained by Katy Cupsworth.

Please welcome from Holland, Delft Dynamoes, captained by Dee Dee Eggers.

Our matches today will be Belmont Avenue v Bruges Braves and Edinburgh Eagles v Delft Dynamoes. The winners will play each other tomorrow in the final of the IT, while both losers will play for third and fourth place.

Finally, this year we once again have various VIPs and scouts from around Europe watching the matches, so who knows, there might be a professional contract or two handed out over the course of the weekend… and my apologies for the smell of rotten eggs, I just don't where it's coming from, but I 'shell' investigate."

All the Belmont team looked at Felicity.

In the Directors' Box sitting in the front row were several celebrities. There was Hans Free the ex-Germany striker who now owned the largest car mobile phone company in the world, Alice Clearr and Cee Frue the married owners of the tournament sponsors, Holland Windows, and Buk End, the shy publishing entrepreneur who was sitting at the end of the front row on his own.

Within minutes the matches kicked off. Katy kicked off their match with a back pass to 'Roly' Paula, so she could get an early feel of the ball. Bruges Braves were a strong team with many skilful players, and it was not long before they were spraying passes all over the pitch. However, for all their undoubted ball skills, they were failing to trouble 'Roly' Paula. They lacked an incisive edge, an ability to make that telling pass or to create an unstoppable shot. This is where Belmont, and in particular Katy, had the edge in the 'Screamer!'

Evie Hazard and the Bruges Braves didn't have to wait long to experience the 'Screamer'. Belmont took a short corner, and Tick Tock Tracey, as she often did, found herself in acres of space on the edge of the box just at the right time. The ball was played to her, but she just stepped over it. She knew Katy was behind her and the rest was history. Katy struck the ball and it flew like a rocket into the top right-hand corner of the net. One nil quickly became two nil. Then two nil became three nil. Belmont were running riot. Katy was loving it and was the centre of attention as most of the play went through her. Evie Hazard, though, was not impressed. She took any defeat personally and when she sensed losing, her aggressive attitude would take over, hence her nickname, 'Evil' Hazard.

With the score at 5-0 and only a few minutes to go, something terrible happened. Katy was lining up another 'Screamer', but just as she was about to launch the ball, 'Evil' Hazard came flying in with an almost waist-high illegal tackle. Katy was sent sprawling to the floor headfirst into the mud. The referee had no choice but to give 'Evil' Hazard a straight red card, which was almost unheard of in the history of the tournament.

As 'Evil' left the pitch in shame, she called out to Katy, "eat mud Cupsworth!"

As Katy got back to her feet, she sensed something was not quite right. Her left leg was numb. She had what seemed like a dead leg which meant she could hardly feel her precious left leg, and this would affect her ability to deliver the 'Screamer.' Tears welled up in her eyes as she feared her tournament would be over barely before it had begun. Felicity had seen that look in Katy's eyes before.

"Ted, Ted, take Katy off now and get Missy on. Katy's hurt!" Felicity shouted.

Ted quickly held up the subs board and Katy slowly limped off, barely looking at Missy.

"It's my leg mum, it's dead. I'm never going to make the final now," said Katy crying into Felicity's arms.

"Katy, let me see what I can do. Here, put this ice pack on it, it will really help," said Felicity trying to console her daughter.

The match had barely re-started when the referee blew his whistle to signal the end of the game. Belmont had won, but it was a bittersweet victory as Katy was injured. With the final being played tomorrow, there was little chance Katy would be fit.

The despondent players and parents drove the short distance to their hotel, unpacked their bags and had dinner in the hotel restaurant, all except Felicity, who headed straight for the Hotel hairdressers!

Delft Dynamoes had dispatched Tania Swift's Edinburgh Eagles 3 – 0 and this wasn't a big surprise as Delft were a top team, had the best player in the tournament in Dee Dee Eggers and were confident they would retain the IT again. All that stood in their way was Belmont Avenue, a team who were thought of as nothing without their inspirational captain, Katy Cupsworth.

The next day, the final kicked off without Katy, who sat all alone on the touchline feeling sorry for herself. She still wanted the team to win, but without her this would surely be impossible. She resigned herself to thinking that losing by a low score was probably the best outcome.

For all the pressure and possession of Delft, it was Belmont who took a surprise lead. Tick Tock Tracey had found herself all alone as she ran on to a pass in the penalty area, but then stopped as she thought she was offside. She playfully kicked the ball into the net expecting the referee to blow for offside. But no whistle came, much to the dismay of Delft Dynamoes, and the clear frustration of Dee Dee Eggers. Belmont were leading one nil.

Upon the re-start, Delft kicked the ball up the pitch towards the Belmont goals. All the Delft players were charging after the ball, all except Dee Dee Eggers. She was a smart player who had a hunch that one of her own players would get to the ball first. Sure enough, Delft retained possession on the edge of the Belmont box.

"On my egg, on my egg Wendy" shouted Dee Dee as her teammate took possession of the ball. "On her egg…..on her egg" chanted the home crowd in reply.

However, the very mention of eggs made Felicity break out in a cold sweat and she started twitching spontaneously. It was a very odd sight indeed.

Back on the pitch, Wendy barely looked up as she knew the call from Dee Dee, and she knew exactly where Dee Dee wanted the ball. Dee Dee was going to 'eggs-sploit' the situation!

Wendy crossed the ball and Dee Dee ran on to it. 'Roly' Paula though had seen her run and went to block any header that Dee Dee could make. The next few seconds not only shocked Paula, but also the whole of the Belmont players and parents.

Just as Dee Dee was about to head the ball, she calmly stooped down, and the ball miraculously nestled in the back of her neck. Rather than heading the ball, she started to carry the ball on her neck around 'Roly' Paula and then bent down and let the ball roll down her shoulders and into the empty net.

Dee Dee had always practised catching an egg on the back of her neck as her dad said all the top footballers could do this. Over the years she had developed this technique and had used it to score many surprising goals.

The Belmont parents went silent, as if in shock. What a brilliant piece of skill and what confidence to try this trick! Belmont Avenue had just witnessed the amazing Dee Dee Eggers famous 'egg trick' and the Delft Dynamoes' supporters started to chant her nickname 'Ego Eggers, Ego Eggers'.

On the chanting of Ego Eggers, Felicity frantically ran for cover, scared that more eggs were about to be thrown at her!

Katy was half in awe of Dee Dee, and half depressed, as now Delft would surely go on and win the match, and retain the IT.

But for all of Katy's doubts, Belmont surprisingly held on to draw 1-1 and now extra time was to be played.

Belmont tried their best, but it was obvious Delft had the better players. Nevertheless, they never gave up. With only a few minutes left, Ted made a risky decision.

"Ref, sub please. Katy you're going on," announced Ted.

"Dad, I'm injured. I can't play!" pleaded Katy.

"Listen Katy, just hop around until we get into the penalty shoot-out. Then you can take a pen and let them see the 'Screamer'" proclaimed Ted who was 100% sure this was a substitution that would win them the game.

Reluctantly Katy limped on. The last place she wanted to be now was on the pitch as she could hardly walk, and she believed that the odds of winning were less than zero. This was negative Katy at her worst, showing no confidence and fearing failure. But could she find something inside her to overcome this predicament?

Her thinking was temporarily cut short as the referee blew the whistle to signal the end of the match. The penalty shoot-out would begin shortly.

"Right girls, gather round, here is the order of the penalties. Carly, Ranvir, Tick Tock, Missy and Katy you take the last pen," said Ted casting an eye at Katy.

"I can't even stand up properly, never mind take a pen!" exclaimed Katy.

Katy, just do your best, that's all we ever want," said Felicity calmly looking at Katy.

Reluctantly Katy nodded her head and the team got ready for the shoot-out to win the IT.

Delft won the toss and decided to kick first. The conditions were not perfect for penalties as a strong wind was starting to blow. Both sets of players were more than a little nervous. Despite this, each player scored their own penalty, with many cleanly dispatched into the net. The score reached 4-4 and in effect it was now sudden death pens. Taking penalty number five for Delft Dynamoes was Dee Dee Eggers.

A big cheer went up from most of the crowd as Dee Dee struck the prefect penalty to make it 5-4 to Delft. Now it was Katy's turn to save the match.

Katy started to lose all her confidence as she sat in the centre circle. She turned away instead to look at the *windmills*. However, what caught Katy's attention was the fact that even though there was now an even stronger wind blowing, the windmills were not turning. This didn't seem right.

"Well, well young Katy, things not turned out the way you expected they would? Has the wind been taken out of your sails, just like at school when you think you can't do something? Better throw in the towel now then?"

"Who said that?" asked Katy turning around quickly to find out who was talking to her. As Katy turned around, the only person she could see was a young lady who couldn't have been that much older than Katy herself, maybe 15 or 16. This young lady was wearing a long white robe with a black rope belt around her waist. She was nearly 6ft tall and was barefoot.

"Ha ha, don't you remember me Katy. Concentrate on my voice. Have you heard it before?" asked the young lady.

Although Katy was in shock, she still managed to think. Where had she heard that voice before?

"Come on Katy, 'wind' back your mind to your first encounter with Meanie Marcie McGhee when you were sitting in the mud, knickers on your muddy head, almost a bit like you are doing now." said the lady almost teasing Katy.

Then Katy recognised the voice and when it had last helped her.

"Fred? That's what you look like is it….you're not a cloud. You're a woman in a karate suit? But isn't Fred a man's name!" said Katy, a little bemused.

"Well done Katy, I underestimated your powers of observation. Yes, it's me and I am here to help. Yes, I am a woman, so well noticed, and no I don't practice karate, although I once wrapped someone up while doing origami!

"Now seriously, all I want to say is be ready and don't be scared of what might go wrong. Think of what could go right. You must show **confidence**, which is not being scared of what people say, or even not being scared of what you think they might be saying. Don't fear Dee Dee, don't fear losing, don't fear fear itself and never let Doubting Debbie get in your head, like that match against Anchor Inn WFC," said Fred looking for a response from Katy.

Katy stood up and walked to the penalty spot and placed the ball on the spot. As she turned around to create her run up, she glanced at the halfway line and something caught her eye. Dee Dee Eggers was jumping up and down almost celebrating victory before Katy had even taken her penalty. As Katy looked for a second longer, all she could see was DD on the back of her shirt. Oh no she thought, it's that Doubting Debbie here to wreck my chances.

"Hold on young Katy, before we go any further, I have a little question for you" said Fred as she instantly got Katy's attention.

"Do you think top footballers lose their confidence before taking a penalty? What about Marta, or the top USA striker Mia Hamm? Or Sun Wen from China, or even our own Kelly Smith?" asked Fred.

Katy knew the answer to that question. All those players were the best in the world and always showed great confidence. They loved the opportunity to be a match winner.

Katy smiled and just nodded in agreement with Fred.

"You must *work it out*" shouted Fred, eager to hep Katy before she took the penalty. Now here are your choices and consequences:"

Katy has three **choices:**

1 Shut your eyes and strike the ball as hard as you can. You might get lucky and score.
2 You decide to use your weaker right foot to try and place the ball in the net. You are too scared to use the left foot 'Screamer'. If you miss, everyone will give you sympathy.
3 Use your nerves to pump yourself up and use your injured left foot to try and deliver the 'Screamer'.

Which choice should Katy make?

Here are the **consequences:**

1 Nerves continue to play a part in pressure situations, and you rely too much on luck rather than believing in your confidence. It all becomes too much for you and you don't enjoy playing.
2 You go for the sympathy vote every time your ability is threatened. You crumble under pressure. People eventually work you out and don't respect you anymore.
3 Once you have overcome your nerves once, it's easier to do it again. You start to create a good footballing habit. Doubting Debbie has difficulty finding you in the future.

Katy had somehow got a new-found sense of confidence and decided to go for Choice 3. She was simply not scared anymore. She decided to ignore Doubting Debbie. She chose to forget about her injured leg. She chose to focus on what could go right, rather than what could go wrong. She chose confidence.

The referee blew the whistle to signal Katy to take her penalty.

Katy wasn't going to let a little injury and that Dee Dee Eggers get the better of her. Katy then started to talk to herself quietly so that nobody could hear her.

"I'm Katy Cupsworth, and whatever that Dee Dee can do, I can do better. Who does she think she is? I'm the best player at this tournament."

Katy then turned to face Dee Dee and called out, "Watch this egg head!"

Katy ran up and struck the ball cleanly, albeit with not quite her usual power. Nevertheless, the ball started to soar into the top left-hand corner of the net. As the ball was almost past the keeper, and about to enter the net, something extraordinary happened. The wind dropped and it slowed down the ball. This allowed the Delft keeper to simply pick the ball out of the air. Delft had won the IT.

For one brief moment, it seemed the whole crowd was screaming for joy, except for a small group of players and parents from England.

Katy was totally dejected. She had given it her best shot and she hadn't let fear get the better of her and she was confident, yet she had lost.

"Hey Katy darling, great penalty, but perhaps a better save?" asked Fred.

Katy looked confused.

"Well you stuck to your guns and didn't let Doubting Debbie get in your head. You believed in yourself and you showed confidence," said Fred looking very wise.

"You said be confident and it will all work out," replied Katy looking at Fred as if she had let her down.

"Yes, and you did everything I asked. But sometimes things don't always go the way we like. Remember this, when we lose, we always learn," exclaimed Fred now with a smile on her face.

"So, Katy, what did you learn today?" asked Fred.

Katy hesitated for a moment.

"Well Fred, I suppose I learned that even though I was confident, I ended up on the losing side."

Fred continued her message.

"Today you did everything right in terms of confidence, yet still lost because I helped the keeper pull off a great save."

"You did what Fred?" asked Katy starting to get really angry, "You're supposed to be on my side."

"Oh, my dear Katy, I am always on your side, but sometimes I have to teach you a lesson even if it's at the expense of the team. That's why I slowed the wind down, to slow the ball down and make it easy to save. A lack of confidence was your issue at first, but you conquered this fear. But sometimes, if you want to be the best, you may just need **smarter confidence**" said Fred.

"What do you mean Fred, smarter confidence?" asked Katy curiously.

"Well, let me put it this way. Believing in yourself and being confident is essential. But if we start to think we are so much better than everyone else, and start to show off, even shout out bad names to people, then that's being arrogant. It can take away your focus. Dee Dee Eggers has great confidence and it helps her a lot. But sometimes she is overconfident, and this can quickly turn into arrogance. This may one day make her lose concentration and focus, especially when she shouts out negative comments. She got away with it today, catching the ball on the back of her neck with her equaliser, and calling out names, but things may turn out differently for her on another day.

"As for you Katy, you may well have to combine your confidence with a little less arrogance if you truly want to become a professional footballer. You see, the best players don't talk about how good they are. Rather, other people do that for them, talking about their qualities and achievements. For example, your qualities are your ball control, and confidence of not being scared, whilst your achievements could be being leading scorer, and being team captain. The great players can use this as confirmation of their ability, yet they never use it to become overconfident or arrogant. They are smart. Get it now Katy?" asked Fred.

Katy nodded.

"But what if you feel you don't have enough confidence, let alone any smarter confidence Fred?" she asked, curiously.

"Well, this is where my **Fred Fix 1 - Balloon Blow & Balloon Pop** come in!" replied Fred.

http://bit.ly/Katyvideo1

FRED FIX

"To build yourself up, simply inflate a balloon to the correct size, and then start writing all of your qualities and achievements on the outside of the balloon, football qualities and achievements, and others outside football, such as having good friends, supportive parents, being kind. Also ask your friends, parents or other family members to write about your qualities and achievements. So then, if you feel a little down because you are letting Doubting Debbie into your head, you will always have something to remind yourself of how much progress you are making.

"Sometimes though, we have barriers which stop us performing. So, instead of writing our qualities and achievements on a balloon, we might want to write down all our barriers, things that are stopping us performing at our best, like nerves or fear of failure. Then we pop the balloon, and very quickly we notice that these barriers have shrunk already as the words on the popped balloon are so much smaller – it's a great start to beating these barriers."

"But what if I can't decide which one to do?" asked Katy curiously.

"That's simple, you do both! But I bet very soon, you won't need to pop or inflate a balloon to show you how much progress you are making…. you will just know," said Fred wisely.

"But don't worry about this now, otherwise you will become deflated!" said Fred, who had started to chuckle at her own jokes. "But, let me tell you, from the first moment I saw you playing football in your back garden, I instantly knew you were going to go far" she continued.

"Hang on a minute. Were you spying on me Fred?" asked Katy angrily.

"I wouldn't call it spying, just keeping a friendly eye on you that's all," replied Fred.

Katy was full of emotions. She was upset because she had lost the game for her team and she was also really angry at Fred for helping their keeper save her penalty. She turned around to give Fred a piece of her mind.

"You're just a joke…." Katy stopped mid-sentence. Fred had completely disappeared, almost as quickly as she appeared a few minutes before.

"Katy, well done. I know the keeper saved your penalty, but it was a great effort to let her have the 'Screamer', even though you were injured," said Felicity proudly.

Katy caught her own angry mood, and with those kind words from her mum, she started to calm down and relax. She had given it her best shot, and even though she didn't like what Fred had done, a small part of her still believed in Fred and her weird ways.

"Well done keeper, great save," said Katy as she shook hands with the Delft keeper.

Felicity went over to Ted and both had to agree that losing wasn't a good feeling, but the way Katy and the team lost was a credit to each and every one of them.

"That was the perfect way to represent England – win, lose or draw, fair play to all," said Felicity sporting her new 'free range' hairstyle.

Mission 2 Questions

- Which country and town did they visit?
- "Win, lose or draw, fair play to all." What do you think this means?
- Why was the beginning of the visit such a disaster for Felicity?
- What is the significance of the windmills, the wind and how this relates to Fred?
- How did Katy's dead leg affect her confidence?
- Why did Fred slow Katy's penalty down?
- Describe what "smarter confidence" is.
- What was the "Balloon Blow"?
- What did Katy learn about confidence?

Key Words

Confidence

Smarter Confidence

Fred Fix 1 - Balloon Blow & Balloon Pop

Global Video Mission 2

http://bit.ly/KatyCupD

— Mission 3 —

THE LIONESS IS BITTEN, BUT WILL SHE BITE BACK?

Dick, Kerr's Girls are resilient and strong,
But when it comes to Katy's reaction, does she get it wrong?
Those qualities will surely lead to success,
Or does she find herself in a mess?

Even though Belmont Avenue didn't win the IT, they still enjoyed the experience and learned loads about football, and about themselves.

Back home, January quickly turned into February, and this year the weather was especially harsh. Several weeks had passed by without any games being played as all the pitches were waterlogged and unplayable. It seemed ages ago since they had last played and that was in Delft.

The bad weather though didn't mean that football completely stopped for Katy. Rather, it meant more practice in the back garden with Chris, and some of the girl players like 'Roly' Paula, and a new girl Ronnie, who had recently joined the team. She had blonde hair in a long ponytail and always had a look of determination on her face – she simply never knew when she was beaten.

Katy instantly took to Ronnie, which was a little strange as they seemed quite opposite in nature, and footballing ability. Ronnie wasn't the best footballer, but her 'never give up at anything' attitude was a quality which Katy quietly admired, and respected.

"Pass Katy, I'm free!" shouted Chris.

"Try and stop this then Cuppa boy!" exclaimed Katy as she slid in a pass to Ronnie with only Chris to beat.

Ronnie took a swing at the ball, but slipped on the muddy makeshift garden pitch. Chris started to laugh and high-fived Paula as they both stood over Ronnie. Katy started to sulk. Ronnie though wasn't beaten just yet. As she was sitting in the mud, she stuck her leg out at an awkward angle, and without fear of injuring herself, or indeed, a fear of failing, she connected with the ball which then catapulted towards the goal line. Before 'Roly' Paula and Chris could react, Ronnie had slid head-first towards the ball and headed it over the line, whilst at the same time covering her face in thick mud. This was Ronnie at her best – she never knew when to quit.

As the weeks passed by, the weather and the condition of the pitches, started to improve slowly. The recent winds had really dried Belmont Rec, and soon the League and Cup competitions could be resumed.

As the season was reaching its climax, the league had become a two-horse race between Belmont Avenue and a team called Dick, Kerr's Girls. DKG, as they were commonly called, had started off the season at the bottom as they had lost their opening five games. They sacked their manager, and William Frankland Junior took control. He instilled a positive team attitude and treated everyone with respect, as long as they worked hard for the team, and didn't try to show off.

DKG slowly started to improve, and started to win most of their matches. They also never gave up, and had rescued many points late in the second half, and even in time added on. They never knew when they were beaten. The team affectionately called this 'Frankland Junior Time.' There were no superstars in the team, just every player giving 100%.

Inevitably, the league decider match, as it had become known, arrived and it was attracting a lot of attention. Both teams had quite a few supporters, and this crowd was boosted by the fact that most of the other matches had been called off at late notice. There was also a rumour that a few professional scouts would be attendance. There was more than air of expectation and excitement surrounding the match.

As both teams lined up on the pitch, Katy noticed two players who shouldn't have been there, but they were! Cunning William Frankland Junior had pulled off a dramatic last-minute transfer which added even more grit to his team. He had signed no other than the Sanchez Sisters. This was the final piece in the football jigsaw for William Frankland Junior and he knew they had the beating of Belmont, and so sadly, did many of the Belmont players. Even Ted and Felicity were not too sure they could win this match.

As the referee blew for kick off, DKG kicked the ball long towards the Belmont area. There was a charge of players from DKG as they descended on their opponents. 'Roly' Paula hesitated as she was about to collect the ball. Panic had set into the whole Belmont defence. 'Roly' hesitantly kicked the oncoming ball, but she mis-kicked it and it sliced into Tick Tock Tracey and rebounded into the Belmont goal. Tick Tock Tracey was, for once, in the wrong place at the wrong time and had scored an own goal.

Most of the crowd on the touchline were jumping for joy and laughing at the sight of such a silly goal to concede. Even the professional scouts seemed to have smiles on their faces. The professional careers of 'Roly' Paula and Tick Tock had been crushed before they had even started.

From the re-start, Katy went on a mazy run as if trying to score single handedly. She went past one, then past two, and the DKG goals were looming large. She was about to unleash her 'Screamer' when she felt her long legs give way underneath her.

The next thing she knew, Katy was on the floor. Sadia Sanchez had 'deliberately by accident' taken her out, by subtly tripping her up and the ref hadn't even blown for a foul.

"Well Katy Cupsworth, you may pass me, the ball may pass me, but never both!" said Sadia as she laughed at Katy sitting in the mud. Katy was getting used to sitting in the mud!

This time, Katy was determined not to give up and decided to take a leaf out of Ronnie's book. Katy ran over to 'Roly' to collect the ball in the Belmont box. Quickly, Katy started to dribble out, but lost control at a vital moment. As the ball rolled loose, Sarina intercepted it, and dribbled towards 'Roly' Paula in the Belmont goal and was about to unleash a shot.

But not deterred by her mistake, Katy slid in at the side of Sarina, and in the blink of an eye, poked the ball away from Sarina's foot just as she was about to shoot. It was a good, clean, fair challenge. But, just as Katy had poked the ball away, two things happened. Firstly, not wanting to lose the opportunity to score, Sarina, fell to the floor, and then secondly, let out a piercing cry of pain, as if she had been fouled. The referee was a little behind play and not quite sure what had actually happened. But so convincing was the fall and cry from Sarina, the ref pointed to the penalty spot – penalty to DKG!

As Sarina got to her feet, she walked across to Katy and whispered, "There is more than one way to win a match…daddy's girl!"

Katy had again been challenged, albeit in a sneaky, cheating way, and had come second best again. Her instinct was to give up, like at school. Or maybe, get angry and seek revenge. As the wind began to pick up again, she could feel tears forming in her eyes.

"Hello, Katy darling, did those sneaky Sanchez Sisters teach you another lesson?" came the familiar voice.

"Not you again Fred, did you do this on purpose again, trying to teach me another lesson like in Holland?" asked Katy angrily.

"No, not at all Katy. I only interfere when I really need to and you're doing so well on your own. But I did want a word with you," replied Fred.

"Hey Fred, is it me, or do you look different, slightly older than when we last met in Delft?" asked Katy curiously. "Or are you not wearing any make-up?" added Katy cheekily, feeling more familiar with Fred.

"I do wear an occasional mud pack to hold back the years, but obviously not as often as you like to use it! Never mind me, this is all about you Katy. I need to tell you a story" exclaimed Fred excitedly.

Fred sat down next to Katy and started to engage her with a story about Dick Kerr.

"You see Katy, Dick, Kerr's Girls has its foundation in Dick, Kerr's Ladies which was a team set up during World War One in 1917. This was a football team made up of all girls and ladies. Originally, they were not that popular, even though they raised money for the war efforts by charging spectators to watch their matches.

"The men looked down on them as they thought a woman's place was in the home. They also thought they were not good enough to play! DKL had difficulty finding teams to play as many girls and women had been put off by the men. Really, though, the men became a little jealous of the women's popularity especially as in 1920, 53,000 supporters packed into Goodison Park to watch one of their matches, and there were another 14,000 supporters locked out."

Fred continued "They had a lot of **resilience**, and not only that..."

"Wait a minute...resilience?" interrupted Katy, "what does that mean....like when Ronnie plays?"

"Yes, exactly like Ronnie. The ladies never gave up, or if they got beaten, they would work out how to beat that team the next time they played them – they were always trying to improve and knew how to adapt. This resilient quality even showed itself when they couldn't find someone to play. They would search for women teams, and on one occasion even went to France to play a French team. They were indeed resilient as they never stopped raising money for war soldiers," exclaimed Fred.

"In fact, they had a striker at this time who was just phenomenal, not unlike you Katy. Her name was Lily Parr and she was an absolute revelation, joining the team at only age 14. Lily went on to score 980 goals in 833 games over the course of a phenomenal 32-year football career. During this time, she showed women twice her age, how to score and how to never give up when things went wrong. Unlike you at school, and sometimes on the pitch" said Fred trying to make her point very clear to Katy.

"However, it was a man called William Frankland who, as their manager, instilled great teamwork and mutual support into the team. They needed this with almost everybody against them. In fact, some people said, that it was this very situation that made the team stronger and enabled them to go on and have so much success on and off the pitch. This 'never say die' attitude has been instilled in Dick, Kerr's Girls now under the guidance of grandson William FranklandJunior."

"How do you know all this Fred?" asked Katy.

"That's easy. When I was younger, I was always interested in facts. I loved finding out stuff, especially if it had anything to do with sport, and especially football. In fact, my nickname in my youth was 'Forensic Fred' as I used to examine loads of football facts and trivia."

"So, a bit of a nerd were you Fred… more like 'Smarty Pants Fred'," said Katy cheekily.

"You know all about pants Bridget Jones, as you wear them on your head during football matches…shall we move on Katy?" said Fred smugly.

"This story is about you. You see, being the best footballer with smarter confidence is a good start, but it is exactly that, just a start. You need to develop this resilient quality if you want the scouts over there to sign you up," said Fred looking across to the touchline.

"In fact, you need to 'fail-forward' rather than 'fail-backward.' By this I mean, when things don't go right, and we fail, the ability to learn from this failure will help you become more resilient next time you are faced with a similar challenge. This is what I mean by 'fail-forward' as opposed to giving up and 'fail-backward.' Now, let's focus on what has happened. Sarina Sanchez has cheated to get a penalty. How do you respond resiliently? Try and *exercise* your brain and don't get *hot-headed*.

Here are your choices and consequences Katy."

Katy has three **choices:**

1 **You moan at the ref and say Sarina Sanchez cheated.**
2 **You decide to get revenge the next time you go past Sarina Sanchez.**
3 **You decide that nothing can be done now, and you make sure Sarina doesn't catch you out again.**

Which choice should Katy make?

Here are the **consequences:**

1   You swear at the referee and get in her face. Your mum and dad both run on to the pitch to calm you down, but the damage has already been done. The referee gives you a straight red card and orders you off the pitch. Sadly, your team gives up as they don't believe they can beat DKG without you.

2   The next time you have the ball, or not, you sneakily elbow Sarina in the face. The referee sees you do this and gives you a straight red card. Sarina isn't impressed and sees you after the match for some 'two on one time' with her sister Sadia! Belmont Avenue eventually lose 5-0 and lose the League to DKG. The professional scouts never return to see you play as they know you have an attitude problem.

3   You accept the referee's decision. Even though your pride hurts, you apologise to your team-mates and work even harder to win the match. Everyone feels like an injustice has happened, but with your apology and your leadership, Belmont are even more motivated to beat DKG - even Sarina is shocked. The scouts start writing positive notes about your resilient character.

As play carried on, Katy did something to get her own back. She picked Choice 2 and sneakily elbowed Sarina in the face. Unfortunately, the referee saw it and had no hesitation in giving Katy a straight red card. Her match was over. Even worse, the scouts were making notes that were probably not too complimentary about her attitude. Too late, Katy reflected that revenge and resilience aren't not the same thing.

With Belmont's star striker off the pith, DKG easily went on to win the match and so collect the League title. Katy was still angry, but her anger changed to fear, as the Sanchez Sisters left the pitch and headed straight over to her. It was going to be a painful lesson for Katy!

On the opposite touchline, FIFA Head Scout Ivor Contract and FIFA Chief Medical Doctor Sir Gerry Mendit, approached Ted.

"Listen Ted, bad news about losing the title. You could have won it if your girl had kept her head and shown some backbone that was within the rules " said Ivor.

"Sorry Mr Contract, it was just one of those days. Katy never usually retaliates like that and….." before Ted could finish his sentence, Sir Gerry interrupted.

"Actually, this is not the first time I have seen her react poorly to a situation that she didn't like. I have had conversations with a couple of her teachers at school, and a couple of coaches, and sadly, this seems to be her Achilles heel, a condition which even I can't fix in surgery!" Ivor carried on where Sir Gerry finished.

THE AMAZING JOURNEY OF KATY CUPSWORTH

"Sometimes when threatened by a situation she does not like, she either gives up, or like today, reacts in the wrong way. She's a good, solid player, but all the pro players I work with must also have resilience. Resilience in challenges, resilience in overcoming injuries, resilience to accepting criticism," said a disappointed Ivor as he walked away from Ted.

Over on the other touchline, Katy was nursing a bruised eye and ribs, courtesy of Sadia and Sarina.

Fred re-appeared as a gentle breeze wafted across the pitch.

"What a great performance Katy!" said Fred.

"We lost, I got an unlucky red card and I played well?" questioned Katy.

"No, not your performance. The performance by the Sanchez Sisters. It was very impressive dealing with you!" said Fred smirking. "You had better see your mum, or better still, maybe you should take a first aid course, so you can treat yourself, as I am sure we haven't seen the last of this negative behaviour," said Fred.

"In fact, even Ronnie or Cuppa could teach you a thing or two about being resilient and choosing the right response," added Fred, looking for any type of response from Katy.

"Listen Fred, the last thing I need now is a lecture from a middle-aged woman. I'm a young super-star striker who is going to play pro footy one day," replied an angry and upset Katy.

"One day might be a long way off Katy," replied Fred, before adding….."unless you develop a stronger character."

"OK then Fred, what do you suggest Mrs Know it All?" asked Katy, who was beginning to feel less annoyed and more interested in what Fred was saying.

"Oh, at last Katy, now you're asking the right question. Now listen carefully. The trick is to **respond** rather than **react**. By this I mean, think about your reaction. Rather than quickly reacting in a moody way, respond positively....unlike how you are with me now!

"Or maybe think of it in terms of colours ie **Green Respond** when you are calmly thinking about what to do, or **Red React** when you quickly rush without thinking.

http://bit.ly/KatyVideo2

"A good example of someone who can do this is the intrepid explorer Randy Finds."

THE AMAZING JOURNEY OF KATY CUPSWORTH

Katy's ears pricked up and she started to listen carefully to Fred's story.

"Well Randy Finds is a famous explorer, and he always finds his destination, hence his name. It's not by luck he always finds the place he is going to either. No, it's down to his ability to use his resilience to survive extreme temperatures, either up a cold mountain, or alone in a hot sun-baked desert.

"He once couldn't use his frostbitten fingers to tie a knot, and was stuck up a mountain on his own. So instead of reacting by panicking, he responded by cutting off a couple of fingers, so he could carry on mountaineering. I don't expect you to do that, though Katy! Randy even had a couple of heart attacks. But rather than let that stop him exploring, he just had a heart bypass operation and carried on a few months later. I don't expect you to do that either Katy."

Katy was starting to feel sick listening to Fred's extreme cases of resilience.

"Calm down Katy, don't react badly. Randy has also responded in less dramatic fashion, more appropriate for you to learn from. For example, if he gets lost, he always re-checks his compass and navigation tools, and if need be, re-sets his course and starts again. Now that's something you can do isn't it, start again, rather than give up?" asked Fred hoping her message was getting through to young Katy.

Katy nodded in agreement.

"How about an example of resilience from Mother Nature?" asked Fred, who had detected Katy was now feeling a little squeamish.

Katy nodded her approval again.

"Resilience is all around us in the outdoors. For example, when a terrible fire ravages a forest, everything is destroyed. Yet often, just a few days later, tree buds can sprout and begin the recovery process of slowly growing into a tree again.

"Similarly, have you ever seen pavements with weeds growing between the cracks in the concrete? The weeds just never give up and keep pushing against the concrete until they find a gap and they eventually breach the concrete surface and take light and rain from the environment.

"Or think about salmon swimming upriver and all the constant challenges they face to get to their breeding grounds, like the current and prowling hungry bears? Or a spider that has its web destroyed by a bird flying into it or a person walking through it….they have to re-build it, sometimes over and over again. It's almost as if it's in their DNA, their own identity. However, sometimes, the ability to keep on trying and never give up may not be enough."

Katy started to frown.

"Hang on a second Katy, I didn't say it's impossible. It's just that sometimes resilience needs to be helped by standing back and reflecting on what needs to be done next to get success.

"A really simple way of demonstrating this **'Reflect' Resilience** is by using a **potato and a straw**," said Fred pausing for a much-needed breath.

http://bit.ly/KatyVideo3

"Now Fred, I get the weeds, salmon and spider stuff, but a potato and a straw?" queried Katy who was anxious to learn more.

"It really is simple Katy. Here, take this potato and try and push the straw right the way through it, to the other side," said Fred offering Katy a small potato and a straw.

"It's impossible Fred, it's bound to fail as the potato is too thick and the straw is very weak," replied Katy, refusing to take on the challenge.

"Just try Katy…and believe you can do it" demanded Fred.

Katy picked up the straw and tried to push it through the potato. It broke instantly. She grabbed another straw and tried again. It failed again. When Katy reached for her third straw, Fred stopped her.

"Katy, I admire your resilience, but maybe now is a good time to use 'reflect' resilience. You simply need some more help and guidance. In this case, try and put your thumb on the top of the straw before you punch it through the potato…and believe it will go through."

Katy picked up her fourth straw, placed her thumb over the end of the straw, and plunged it into the potato. It barely touched the sides, as it slid through and came out the other side….success!

"This quality of 'reflect' resilience is the quality you must develop if you want to become a pro footballer. Now, let's get back to where we were Katy, and give you the specific tools to respond to the Sanchez Sisters. This is a good time for my **Fred Fix 2 - Elastic Band Flick**."

http://bit.ly/KatyVideo4

So, whether you like it or not Katy, here it is. In terms of your football situation, when Sarina won the penalty, you should have thought how to beat her next time in a footballing sense, rather than a physical sense. And anyway, she still got you after the match!"

Katy was now nodding in agreement whilst at the same time feeling her 'Sanchez' wounds.

"So, here is what I suggest you do on the pitch next time you are challenged, to show some resilience," added Fred.

Katy's eyes widened as she was now listening intently to Fred's wise words.

"Why don't you wear an elastic band on your wrist, even have one to tie back your hair. Failing that, just use the knicker elastic that you like to wear on your head…ha, ha. Seriously though, when you are physically challenged, or even verbally, just flick the elastic band to give you a quick pang of pain. This will instantly remind you to respond properly by thinking about the right response, rather than simply reacting in an angry way," added Fred, noticing her words were having a positive effect on Katy.

FRED FIX

"It works even better when you breathe in deeply, count to three, and then breathe out for three. So, next time you are challenged, use your resilience to fight back, but not literally fight back!" quickly added Fred, before suudenly disappearing again.

"Katy, we're over here, time to get changed and go home" called out Felicity.

Katy wandered over to Felicity, and caught Ted's eye. Ted was neither sad or happy, just a little down as he had seen his hopes for Katy take a bit of a knock.

"Never mind Katy, you might get another chance one day" he said, rueing the lost opportunity.

Mission 3 Questions

- What qualities did Ronnie have?
- Who were Dick, Kerr's Ladies and what qualities did they have?
- What is the difference between react and respond?
- Why are the scouts reluctant to sign Katy?
- Why was Randy Finds a good role model?
- What was the "elastic band flick"?
- What do you understand by the term resilience?
- What is the significance of "exercise" and "hot headed"?
- Did Katy show resilience? Explain your answer.

Key Words

Resilience	Respond v React
Fail Forward	Green Respond v Red React
Fail Backward	'Reflect' Resilience (a potato & a straw)
Achilles Heel	Fred Fix 2 – Elastic Band Flick

Global Video Mission 3

http://bit.ly/KatyCupE

Mission 4

THE LIONESS UNDERSTANDS 'VOLLEY WELL' ON THE BEACH

Volleyball is a team game,
Will Katy make a mistake and start to blame?
Katy must learn to understand individual need,
Or will she do a bad deed?

U nsurprisingly, Katy couldn't sleep that night at Ted's house. Partly because it was a hot night, and the cooling bedside fan was quite noisy, and partly due to the thoughts of her sending off, which were still whizzing around in her head. Or it could have been the bruising, which was appearing all over her body, courtesy of the Sanchez 'experience'.

She had let down her parents and teammates, and was also disappointed to have let down the FIFA Head Scout and Doctor. She felt she had ruined her chances of a professional footballing career.

Tears started to roll slowly down her cheeks as she continued to reflect on her silly actions. Katy was used to be being the centre of attention, but this sort of attention was unwanted, and now she had to live with the consequences of her actions. She had brought it all on herself.

It was midnight when the church bells softly chimed outside her bedroom window, disturbing her sleep. As she dozily sat up in bed, all she could hear was the whirling of the fan's blades which created a light breeze.

"Wakey wakey, Katy Katy. Get your clothes on, we are off," shouted Fred, appearing out of nowhere to bark out her orders.

"Hey Fred, will you ever give me a break? If it's not on the football pitch, then it's in my sleep. What do you want this time?" said Katy frantically quizzing Fred.

"I'm taking you to a far-away place, to learn some more things, just like I did in my younger days, on my *learning journeys*" replied Fred with a huge smile on her face.

Reluctantly, Katy agreed to accompany Fred.

"Shall I pack some clothes and stuff now Fred?" asked Katy, nervous about what lay ahead. "Will I need my kit and footy boots Fred? Where are we going in the middle of the night? Can't it wait until tomorrow? I don't want to upset dad, and when mum finds out I have gone, she will ground me for a month!" squeaked Katy fearful of the consequences.

"Listen Katy, all will be revealed very soon. Don't worry about dad and mum, I will speak to them. As for your kit and footy boots, they are the last things you will be needing," replied a wise Fred, who was rubbing her hands together, loving the way her plan was coming together.

Fred grabbed Katy's hand, and as soon as she did, Katy felt a strange calmness come over her. She then started to feel drowsy and quickly drifted off to sleep in the safe arms of Fred.

"Hey Katy, wake up again. We are in Rio, Brazil and somebody wants to meet you. It's your hero, Marta!" exclaimed Fred.

Marta looked right at Katy.

"Thanks Fred, I can take over from here" said Marta, as Fred quickly disappeared from view. Marta was about to unleash her own questions upon Katy.

"So, this is the Katy Cupsworth I have been hearing so much about is it? Do you really want to learn about becoming a top player in a top team?"

Katy was too shocked to speak. Marta drew a quick breath and carried on.

"And about how you, Katy Cupsworth, can make a difference? Maybe learn about consequences of your actions, like the unfortunate red card you got yesterday?" asked Marta, as she looked for a response from a dazed Katy.

Katy's mind instantly remembered the Sanchez incident.

"Yes, if that's what you think is important. But can you also show me how you score those fabulous goals with your 'Screamer'?" asked Katy with an eagerness in her eyes.

"Scoring goals will be the last thing you need to think about today!" said Marta putting Katy firmly in her place.

Marta led Katy down to the famous Copacabana Beach. The beach was well-known for its golden sands and perfect views, and often hosted many celebrities. Today was a hive of activity as it was very busy with many families playing by the shore and a host of fun beach games going on. Marta & Katy both sat down on the warm sands. The sun shone brightly in the sky and a gentle sea breeze lapped the waves on to the shore.

"Today Katy, we are going to learn about understanding in a team, and understanding as a coach or manager. We won't be using a football, and we certainly won't be sharing the secrets of my 'Screamer'," said Marta, almost sternly.

"What, no football, and no 'Screamer'? Why bother!" said Katy about to go into a full-on strop.

"Well, well, I can see why the ref gave you a red yesterday. You have a rebellious streak in you Katy. The way this is showing itself now will not only harm your football career, but it will also affect your friendships, and your future life, whether that is in football or not," lectured Marta.

"What's this with adults always lecturing me….teachers, parents, Fred and now even my favourite player?" asked Katy.

Marta gave Katy a long, hard stare.

Katy had been put in her place by her hero and it had an immediate effect. Katy reflected on her actions the previous day and slowly it was dawning on her. She had to change, and change fast, for the sake of everything she cared about in her life.

"Now Katy, I want to tell you a story about what happened in Brazil," said Marta, who now had Katy's full attention.

"2016 was the year, and it was the turn of my country, to host the Olympic Games. A sport I was particularly interested in was Women's Hockey. The overwhelming favourites were Holland, which is a place you don't have fond memories of I believe?" asked Marta with a knowing smile.

Marta continued with Katy's eyes fixed firmly on her.

"Throughout the competition, England played well and topped their group with five wins out of five. As they entered the knock-out stages, their confidence was sky high. Yet there was a nagging doubt. Even if they were to win each knock-out match, they would probably meet Holland, the reigning world champions in the final. Holland had also won the Olympic Gold medal in the past two Olympics." explained Marta.

"So, did they reach the final? Did they play Holland?" asked Katy excitedly.

"Yes, and yes. The final was a very tense affair. It ended 3-3 in normal time and went to penalties. In the end England won the penalty shoot-out, unlike your penalty exploits in Delft, and became Olympic Champions for the first time!" exclaimed a now excited Marta.

"Wow, beating the World and Olympic champions was almost unbelievable wasn't it?" asked Katy looking for an answer, even as to reason why England won.

"The Dutch team failed to score a single penalty due to the great saves made by the England keeper Maddie Hinch. But England were more than a one-player team. There was a great team spirit about England. It was this spirit that carried them through to penalties, and eventually to win. But interestingly, after the tournament, it emerged that not all the England players got on with each other off the pitch.

"Yet, such was the team spirit and desire to win, that players never fell out on the pitch and worked together, even though some of them were not best friends," said Marta looking directly at Katy.

Slowly it dawned on Katy.

"So, do you mean that the players learned to work together for the sake of the team's success?" asked Katy.

"It was more than that. They developed a **team empathy**, an understanding of each other's needs, their strengths and weaknesses, and supported each other, irrespective of their personal feelings for each other.

"Not only that, each player made sure they were not involved in any personal grudges with the opposition. A costly sin bin or red card would have put victory in serious jeopardy. It was this 100% professional approach that created a winning team dynamic," said Marta enthusiastically.

Katy stopped asking questions and reflected on what Marta had just said.

In that very moment it dawned on Katy again. Her red card for reacting rashly, rather than responding appropriately, may have cost her the chance of becoming a pro footballer, but it had also affected the whole team too.

"Anyway Katy, enough of the lecture, how about we go and watch the beach volleyball game at the far end of the beach? They tip off in an hour and I had better be there. I'm the coach!" said Marta as she walked off, with Katy in tow.

Despite the blustery conditions, there was an exciting match about to be played between a German side called Tiem Bild, and Marta's team which was made up of big hitting superstar players from USA and Brazil called United States of Brazil.

USB as they were known, were a team who had won many 'memorable' matches because they knew how to 'stick' together as a team. However, they had two players, who each wanted to be the star player of the team – Brazilian Poolinho and USA player 'Oney' McEnroe – these players kept Marta on her toes as they were always competing to be the team match winner.

Poolinho 'Bop Plop' had an impressive 'bop' volley which she used to good effect at the net to win points. However, she had a more effective 'plop' shot, an impressive disguised drop volley which would plop gently over the net to win many points from an unsuspecting opposition. She deployed this sometimes instead of slamming a 'bop' volley over the net.

'Oney' also had a powerful net spike volley in her locker, but it was her monster power serve which she was famous for. It would often go unreturned and just this one serve had won many points for the team, hence her nickname.

The match was quite close and a mistake either way could cost one side victory. With the score tied at 14-14 in the deciding set, it was the turn of 'Oney' McEnroe to serve for USB. She threw the ball in the air and leapt up to connect mid-air. Her enormous hand made contact with the volleyball. The ball rocketed over the net, and gathering pace, hit the sand and bounced so high it was impossible to return.

As 'Oney' turned around to receive the high fives from her team, the umpire intervened.

"Out, 15-14, match point to Tiem Bild."

'Oney' went ballistic with the umpire.

"You can't be serious! You have got to be kidding me. That ball was in," stormed 'Oney', staring at the umpire with a look that could kill from a thousand paces.

Poolinho intervened by calling a time out.

"The umpire called out, so there's no point in arguing," shouted Marta from the touchlines.

The team rushed over to the side of the court and readiness for a team talk from Marta. Marta then motioned Katy across.

"Katy, why don't you give USB a team talk. See if you can show some **leader empathy** for their situation, yet still get them to re-focus and win the match. Sometimes, this means saying things that may be unpleasant for some people to hear, but necessary," said Marta putting Katy right on the spot.

"I learned from many great coaches such as Pia Sundhage and Jill Ellis. They seemed to always win medals when it counted, either at the Olympics or World competitions. They just knew how to get the key information across to the players, at the right times," concluded Marta, who was now looking for a response from Katy.

"Hey Marta, nobody said anything about being a coach. I'm a player you know," fumed Katy, half nervous about addressing the team, and half upset that Fred wasn't there to guide her, just when she needed her most.

"Ok Katy, I thought you were up to it, but I must have been wrong," replied Marta who was starting to get the girls in a group huddle for her team talk.

The wind was now gusting, and the court flags were blowing wildly on each end of the net. Suddenly, a gust of wind blew off Katy's hat. As she bent down to pick it up, she noticed someone looking at her.

It was Fred.

"You took your time. Well, you're too late, Marta is doing the team talk now. Anyway, what could you show me about being a coach?" said Katy, still upset with Fred.

"There you go again, blaming others when really you should be looking at taking the opportunity to do the team talk. If you really want to be a pro player, one day you might have to lead others, and sometimes you will certainly have to talk to your players. Just exactly the opposite of what you're showing me now," said Fred, challenging Katy to respond.

Before Katy could come back at her, Fred was laying down another great learning point.

"Like I am doing with you now, I always try to see the best in everyone. I try and understand their needs and balance this out against the needs of the team. Sometimes you might not be popular, but your job is to be honest and understanding, even if this might offend some people. Those sorts of people will have to learn to take **constructive criticism** if the team is to be successful. If you can't do this, it might be because you have let Doubting Debbie in your head again?" asked Fred assertively, but with a little compassion.

Katy started to think.

"Ok Fred, you have convinced me, I suppose. If I am to develop as a player, especially as I am a captain, I will have to speak to the team and show some empathy, but still be honest, and not let Doubting Debbie affect me?" asked Katy.

Fred nodded.

"Marta, can I have a word with the players please?" asked Katy walking towards Marta and the team huddle.

"Right," said Fred. "Quick. I'm going to set up some choices. Don't get *caught-cold* thinking about it too much.

Here are your choices and consequences:"

Katy has three **choices:**

1   Criticise 'Oney''s attitude and give her some honest constructive criticism.
2   Tell the team they are doing great and just to hang in there.
3   Suggest a different way to respond to the ref's call.
What choice should Katy make?

Which choice should Katy make?

Here are the **consequences** :

1   You come down hard on 'Oney' and tell her to be a team player. 'Oney' doesn't like your words and storms off the beach.
2   The team instantly like you, but the problem has not been solved. 'Oney' tries to make amends by smashing the next flighted ball but misses and loses the match for the team single handed! You are scared of what the players might say if they didn't like what you said. You have let Doubting Debbie get inside your head.
3   You ask 'Oney' to forget about the bad call. You ask her to respond by focusing on the next point by trying to set up Poolinho at the net. This would prove she is a team player after all. 'Oney' sets up Poolinho to win the next point and the match is tied again. You understand 'Oney's actions and saw the best in her.

"Great team talk Katy," said Marta looking a little envious of the effect Katy had on the team. Katy had picked Choice 3 and it was a great choice as USB immediately scored the next point to level the match at 15-15.

Tiem Bild then made an uncharacteristic error on service and handed the initiative back to USB. The score was now 16-15 to USB – match point.

Tiem Bild returned the next service, but USB managed to dig the ball back. 'Oney' again put Katy's words of advice into action and set up Poolinho. But instead of using her 'bop' volley, she used her famous 'plop' shot. The ball dropped over the net and hit the sand to win the match for USB.

The crowd didn't shout 'Poo bop' - unfortunately, it was her other nickname, 'Poo plop' which the crowd loved to shout out.

"Poo plop…….Poo plop…..Poo plop…"and the crowd started to find its voice.

"We love you Poo plop …..we do,
We love you Poo plop …..we do,
We love you Poo plop …..we do
Oh, Poo plop we love you."

Soon the court was full of Poo (plop).

Marta and her team were jubilant, and everyone was hugging 'Plop' and 'Oney'. They did make a good team when they were empathetic to each other.

"Hey Katy, do you want to come and celebrate with us?" asked Marta.

"I'm ok Marta, I need to talk to someone very close to me now," said Katy.

"Oh well, as long as you're ok. You did well today Katy, I have a good feeling about your journey," said Marta waving goodbye.

Fred put an arm around Katy.

"Well Katy, that was a good lesson for you today and we had a laugh too, although I don't recommend you using that Poo Plop chant back home! I'm sure there will be opportunities in the near future to put today's learning into practice in a football match," said Fred, speaking as if she knew something that Katy didn't.

"But you will have to be braver, as the next time you let Doubting Debbie affect your judgment, there could be more significant consequences," warned Fred.

This was a clear warning to Katy – but would she heed this warning in the future? "However, all you need now is **Fred Fix 3 – Eat The Burger!**"

http://bit.ly/KatyVideo5

FRED FIX

"What is it this time Fred?" asked Katy becoming tired with all the lectures.

"Here it comes. My Fred Fix is to always remember that empathy is understanding the needs of the whole team, but it is also understanding the need for players to take criticism constructively without thinking about Doubting Debbie. The best way to do this is to eat a burger," said Fred.

"A burger?" asked Katy looking confused.

"Yes, a burger has a piece of bread on both sides. The bread can be seen as something nice to say. The burger, the meat of the matter in the middle, is when something open and honest has to be said. You know constructive criticism. Finish off with the bread again by adding something nice to finish off with. I also call this the good-bad-good burger!" said Fred, watching to see if Katy understood her Fix.

Katy sort of understood.

"It's a lot to take in, but hopefully you won't get indigestion," joked Fred laughing at her own humour.

"Well, it looks like my time is up on Copacabana Beach Katy, I must dash," said Fred hurriedly as she started to make tracks to leave.

Katy started to feel sad, and a little lonely.

"Why do you have to leave now Fred?" asked Katy with a tremble in her voice.

"For starters, my make-up isn't doing me any favours. I seem to have aged almost overnight. I need to get ready for another of my learning journeys," said Fred excitedly.

"But don't you worry about me young Katy, I would be more concerned about your next little adventure."

"What adventure Fred?" asked Katy who was nearly in floods of tears.

"Don't fret child, I would never leave you all alone. My friend is going to look after you. She has another amazing journey for you. The Sun is going to shine on you again Katy, and very soon," said Fred as she waved goodbye and drifted slowly out of view.

An athletic lady peaked out from behind where Fred had stood and offered her hand to Katy. It was no other than Sun Wen, the world-famous Chinese footballer.

Mission 4 Questions

- In which city and country is Copacabana Beach?
- How did England's Hockey Team show empathy?
- Describe the characters 'Oney' and 'Poolinho'.
- What is constructive criticism?
- Describe the Fred Fix – Eat the Burger.
- What did Katy learn in Brazil?
- How is Fred's character developing?
- What do you understand about the term 'empathy'?

Key Words

Team Empathy	Constructive Criticism
Leader Empathy	Fred Fix 3 – Eat The Burger

Global Video Mission 4

http://bit.ly/KatyCupF

Mission 5

THE TOWERING LIONESS FINDS HER ABILITY TO ROAR

Attitude is everything, with it you've a hope,
Without it, you're a dope,
Whether you become a footballer or not,
With it you can become someone who can't be stopped.

"**N** ow my child, grab my hand, close your eyes, and……. pray!" said Sun Wen.

"Whoa, what do you mean, pray?" asked Katy nervously.

"Listen, you will just have to trust me. Besides, you really don't have a choice," replied Sun Wen taking charge, just like she did on the football pitch.

Katy felt an acceleration of speed throughout her whole body, as if she was being transported. Within what felt like a few brief seconds, she had come to a standstill and was hesitant to open her eyes to find out where she was.

"Now, what do you see child?" asked Sun Wen.

Slowly Katy opened her eyes and was instantly surprised. She was in a room with over fifty young children in what looked like some sort of school, although not like the schools in England. It was more like a big wooden barn with a steel floor, with very little natural light. It felt quite cold.

As she looked more closely, she noticed that not one of the children had looked up. Each and every one was totally engrossed in some sort of writing task. The room was deathly quiet, and you could have heard a pin drop.

Katy felt obliged to remain quiet herself, although she did feel it was a bit geeky. Sun Wen then took her to another room next door. Here she noticed that the children were in groups of three and each group had a box of materials on their own table. For a good few minutes, each child studied what seemed like a set of instructions. Then a bell went off, and the children started to talk to each other quietly, but purposefully. Then another bell rang, and each group of three started to build a sort tower from the equipment in the box.

Slowly, the groups started to construct their own towers, and after a few more minutes, the towers were all starting to look very impressive. All were quite tall, with some more sturdier than others. Finally, another bell sounded, and each group sat down as a team of adults, probably teachers, walked around measuring the height of each tower.

After each tower had been measured, the adults kicked one leg of the table. Some collapsed, and some didn't. The children of the towers that remained upright were excused from the room. The children whose towers collapsed started to study the instructions again. It seemed they would have to re-build their towers.

"What's really going on down there Sun Wen?" asked Katy, not quite understanding what she was seeing.

"Each group has to build a tower over two metres high and it has to withstand a teacher kick test, like simulating an earthquake against a tower block."

"A kick test….it wouldn't survive my left foot 'Screamer' Sun Wen!" replied Katy.

"Let me finish Katy," said Sun Wen impatiently…. "the purpose is to allow children to study the construction instructions alone, then to share their views, and finally they have to build a tower together that can withstand a teacher induced earthquake.

"We are teaching them about following instructions, about sharing knowledge and ideas, and then how to re-build the tower if it collapses. The groups who are successful go to lunch and get to choose the best meal options. The next groups have fewer choices, and the group that comes last has no choice!"

"That sounds a bit harsh, Sun Wen?" said Katy who was starting to feel sorry for the final group.

"Harsh maybe, but it is a great learning lesson. It does put pressure on children to concentrate and work as a team to construct a solid tower, but all we are really doing is preparing them for life beyond school," replied Sun Wen adamantly.

Before Katy could say anything, Sun Wen continued.

"You see, here in China, we try and get children to develop their own abilities. We do this by getting them used to failure, so we can help them deal with it by learning from mistakes, getting support from each other, showing courage to take a few learning risks, and really challenging them to think under pressure to get the right result. So, yes, harsh, but necessary if you want to go out into the world and be a success in whatever you decide to do," said Sun Wen, who was now staring at Katy, making her more than a little uncomfortable.

"We have lessons six days a week, from 8am to 5pm when school ends," added Sun Wen.

"Wow, that's a long day, so intense, Sun Wen. When do they get to play out with their friends?" asked Katy.

"Once they arrive home, they are required to complete two hours of homework, so maybe around 7pm they can play out for a while!"

"Now that is harsh. I would hate to go to that school!" said Katy, almost thankful of her school in Belmont.

"Well, it's not really a choice. The parents also totally support the idea of pushing their children to do their best, to help them find out what they are good at and achieve their potential in life. We believe everyone has ability; they just need to work hard to find it. When they find one talent, they generally find another nearby. So, you see, school is where it all begins. Whether you want to be an actor, a police officer, a politician, or even a footballer, you must develop those **ability mindset skills** at school," said Sun Wen pointing at Katy.

"But I'm not so good at school stuff," said Katy apologetically.

"Not so good ......yet, which means you just need to put more effort in and stop blaming others when things don't go your way. It just might take time, but you will get there eventually. "

"Hang on a minute Sun Wen....I feel a rap coming on, and it may go to No 1, but not quite yet," said Katy trying to be clever.

Before Sun Wen could respond, Katy had put the final touches to her new rap, quicker than her 'Screamer'.

"If you can't do it – Don't fret!
Just add our friend – The word Yet.
Sun Wen, who I have just met
Will help my football ability - I bet."

Not wanting Katy to be the boss, Sun Wen replied...

"Now, now Katy, that's all well and good,
But you have misunderstood,
School is where we learn to be our best,
So, we can pass life's test."

Katy didn't like being challenged, but found another verse...

"Sun Wen I now get ya – it's not all about the soccer,
I gotta look inside, to make myself proper
I have gotta work harder and smarter in school
This is now going to be my golden rule."

"Hey enough of this voice rap, now use your ears to complete your learning Katy!" said Sun Wen wanting Katy to listen.

"When you start to add the word *yet*, your teachers will support you even more, you will start to understand your potential, you will learn from mistakes, even start to love your mistakes as it shows you are learning. So, rather than say fail, how about saying it's **Success-Not-Yet**? Anyway, FAIL means First Attempt In Learning, and when we try again, we do so with more wisdom. Ultimately, your abilities will emerge which you can apply to any profession in life," said Sun Wen hoping that Katy had finally got the message.

Katy had a magical look on her face, as if she had just found out a big secret to her future success. Maybe she had got school and football all wrong. Maybe she needed to develop herself more at school, and then this would help her footballing progress.

"Listen Katy, to stand any chance of being a pro footballer, you will need to demonstrate to the pro club that you are more than a girl who has a few tricks and can score a 'Screamer'. So many young girls have all the skills and tricks these days, but how many have the mindset ability to learn from failure, to keep pushing themselves and be open to guidance? You must knuckle down at school and show all those scouts that you take school seriously."

Katy went silent. It was as if the penny had dropped. Ability was more than just physical ability.

"Another reason I wanted to show you the benefit of an ability mindset is that the chances of you becoming a pro footy player playing in the WPFL is less than 1%. So many try, but don't succeed. Whether it is down to injury, bad attitude, lack of consistent ability, a manager's player preference or whatever, your chances are slim.

"Even the ones who make the grade, their football career might be 15 years at the most, and what do you do with the rest of your life after football? So, why not prepare yourself now with an ability mindset that will serve you all your life. That way you can't lose!" said Sun Wen who was now smiling at Katy.

A car horn blew outside – a taxi had arrived.

"Now Katy, let's go and see a real tower. Shanghai Tower please driver," said Sun Wen asking the driver to take them downtown.

The driver drove them to the Tower which was 632 metres (2073 ft) high. They then took the escalator to the roof top.

It was very windy outside, and the building felt like it was swaying in the wind. "Are we safe up here, Sun Wen?" asked Katy nervously.

"As safe as a tower block in an earthquake," said Sun Wen, who started to laugh at her own joke.

"Seriously, building towers in school is one thing, but being at the top of a tilting tower is completely different," said Katy holding tightly to Sun Wen.

"Ok Katy, no need to hold on to me. Better still, why don't you hold on to this abseil rope. It's going to take you down to the bottom!" shouted Sun Wen above the noisy wind.

Sun Wen stepped outside on to the rooftop terrace and shouted to Katy above the wind.

"Now is the time to prove you have the ability to get down to the bottom without the use of the escalator Katy. See you at McDonald's Golden Arches at the bottom. Last one down buys…double cheeseburger for me Katy," said Sun Wen as she launched herself off the top of the Shanghai Tower.

Katy was so nervous now that she went into a sort of trance, almost unable to speak or even think. She was in panic mode. The golden arches of McDonald's at the bottom looked like two Ds – Doubting Debbie! Katy looked at the doors leading to the elevator, and safety.

It was starting to become even windier, and just at that very moment, a helicopter magically appeared on the roof of the Shanghai Towers, its blades churning the air around creating more gusts of wind.

Then a familiar voice interrupted Katy's panicking. It was Fred.

"Did you read that book, *The Wind in the Willows?* Maybe you prefer the song *Blowing in the Wind,* or that film, *Air Force One*?" asked Fred.

Katy was not amused.

"What's jumping off the Shanghai Tower got to do with playing professional football Fred?" asked Katy who was now getting really nervous.

"I just want to test your ability mindset, to see if you have what it takes to be a success in life, footballer or not," said Fred, challenging Katy.

Katy was now looking very pale, and more than a little confused. Then strangely, Katy started to get angry, very angry.

"Actually, you do remind me a little of someone else who has a bit of an anger issue,"v said Fred. "The only difference is that she uses it to help her achieve her goals. Have you ever heard of the top tennis player, Serenada Williams?

Katy shook her head.

"Serenada would often get upset in matches. Sometimes it would be a poor shot, while at other times, it would be a poor call by the umpire or line judge. Either way she would lose it. She soon realised that if she remained angry, she would continue to play poorly and lose points, even lose the match.

"She decided to channel this emotion by singing a little song to herself. This allowed her to focus her anger on winning the next point, and the next, and the next, until she eventually won the match. In some ways, she was a bit like 'Oney' McEnroe," said Fred smiling to herself as she 'served up' another lesson to Katy.

Fred *wincked* at Katy.

"So, Katy, remember, it's not a *Con*, and you must not *vent* your anger on me. Just make your choices now, but don't forget about the consequences:"

Katy has three **choices** :
1   You have nothing to prove, swear under your breath and storm off back inside the Tower.
2   You listen carefully to the advice of the instructor and attempt the abseil.
3   You freeze at the top even though an instructor is there to help you.

Which choice should Katy make?

Here are the **consequences** :

1   You instantly lose your nerves as you get angry. You tell Doubting Debbie to do one and get lost. You tell Sun Wen you have nothing to prove to anyone and walk back inside the Tower. You lose the learning opportunity to prove people wrong about you being unable to perform under pressure, like when you dribbled too wide around M3 and didn't score.
2   You step over the edge, and see it as an opportunity, not a threat. By dismissing Doubting Debbie, and with the support of Sun Wen, you find your ability to abseil improving. Half-way down the building, you start to enjoy the experience and do a Serenada Williams and start singing the Rod Stewart song, 'We are abseiling, we are abseiling, all the way down the Tower.'
3   You are taken inside the Shanghai Tower and meet up with some of the school pupils. Some laugh at you as you never really tried. You will never find your talents if you never try. Your new BFF is Doubting Debbie, and she never leaves your side!

Katy started to get angry and was swearing under her breath. She picked Choice 1. Her anger stopped her realising that this was a great opportunity to develop her abilities in abseiling. In a sense, she had at least beaten Doubting Debbie. This was the only positive to the situation. Her angry mindset didn't allow her to grow.

Inside the Tower, the familiar voice again of Fred was heard again.

"On the plus side, you didn't let Doubting Debbie get inside your head, so I must applaud you Katy, but…" before Fred had finished her sentence, Katy had interrupted her.

"I know, I missed the chance to test myself. You don't need to remind me, Fred," said Katy dejectedly.

"On the contrary Katy, you might have missed one opportunity, but you did demonstrate your inner passion. We can work with that. If you can learn from your mistakes, and control this anger, it will only be a matter of time before your abilities start to improve," said Fred, raising Katy's spirits.

"Maybe this is a good time for my **Fred Fix 4 - Amy Buster & Star Trek Fingers.** So, whether you like it or not Katy, here it is.

"We are always developing as people, and often this development is at its strongest and best while we are growing up at school. So, we need to take advantage of this situation before we lose the opportunity forever.

"Anger is an emotion that can be useful if it is channelled into helping us achieve our goals. There is a part of our brains called the 'Amygdala', or Amy as I call her. This is the seat of all of our emotions. Whilst some anger can help us do stuff, by overcoming nerves for example, too much can stop us using our brains to make the right calls, the right decisions.

"So, we can either sing a little song to ourselves like Serenada, or we can do the Amy Buster. The next time you feel the anger rising, like the mercury in a thermometer, try and use it by imagining Amy as an angry girl who just needs a bit of help. Simply breathe in and at the same time imagine Amy starting to smile just a little. Then breathe out, and at the same time, think about Amy with a really big smile on her face. Try this three times.

"Or, we can do the Star Trek Fingers. It's almost the same as the Amy Buster, but as we breathe out, think of a time when you were awesome. Then, at the same time, squeeze your index finger and thumb together on both hands. This creates an ideal state for performance, like you're saying to yourself that you're ready."

http://bit.ly/KatyVideo6

Katy tried both the Amy Buster and Star Trek Fingers and instantly recognised that these could really help her.

Fred interrupted her practising, which was a habit Katy had almost come to expect from Fred.

"Well done for now, but I am hoping for better in the near future," said Fred wisely.

"Let's take one final trip together in my helicopter. How about you join me at my favourite learning journey destination in the whole world?

"Pilot, please take Katy to…."

Mission 5 Questions

- Can you name the city and country where Mission 5 is set?
- What was Sun Wen trying to teach Katy?
- What are the "ability mindset" skills?
- In Mission 5, when did Katy show nerves?
- What did Katy learn about Serenada Williams from Fred?
- What is the Fred Fix – Amy Buster?
- Why are the words "con" and "vent" separate?
- What was the significance of the helicopter blades chopping up the air and what happens next?

Key Words

Ability Mindset Skills   Fred Fix 4 – Amy Buster & Star Trek Fingers

Success-Not-Yet

Global Video Mission 5

http://bit.ly/KatyCupG

Mission 6

THE MINDFUL TIBETAN LIONESS PROWLS WITH PRIDE

How we deal with stress determines when we win,
If stress becomes the victor, all our dreams go in the bin,
We can either choose to respond well, or be mad,
But if we get stressed and angry, we will always end up sad.

The helicopter touched down on a remote hillside. The blades of the helicopter slowly came to a standstill and something immediately grabbed Katy's attention. It was quiet. There was a real calmness to everything with only a barely detectable breeze that gently brushed against her skin.

A few sparse buildings were dotted around the hillside, and above these were several mountain ranges that seemed to stretch on endlessly into the distance.

This felt like a special place indeed, a type of place that Katy had never encountered before.

A solitary bell rang out, and within a few brief seconds, about ten men appeared dressed in black robes. Nobody spoke a word as they bowed their heads to Katy, and then offered her some food and a drink.

Another bell sounded, and this time a small man with sunglasses in a white robe appeared. He was quietly singing to himself.

"Welcome to Tibet Sister Katy. I am Buddha Holly. We have been expecting you here at our Tibetan monastery. But before we start to help you Katy, you must leave all your negative thoughts and emotions, including anger, behind. To do this we have a simple technique called the **Monk's Temple** and it goes like this:

http://bit.ly/KatyVideo7

"Whenever you feel anger or are scared, and a negative thought pops into your head, you can eliminate this thought by seeing the Monk's Temple as your place of sanctuary, your safe place. For example, you can see this negativity as a visitor to the Monk's temple. You allow it to knock on your door, and when you answer, you simply tell the visitor to go away and be gone.

"If this visitor is a little more persistent, you invite it into the Monk's Temple. Let it roam around each of your rooms for a minute. Once you have allowed this to happen, you order it to leave by the back door and never return. Both ways work to dispel negativity, but you must practise 'everyday' to become a master!" said a humming Buddha Holly.

Katy did as she was told and practised the Monk's Temple and surprisingly, her tension and anger disappeared.

"Now, how can we help you reach your goals in life?" asked Buddha Holly.

"I really don't know. This is all new to me," said Katy unsure of what she was supposed to say.

"Well, everyone is on a journey in life and my job is to help you achieve your goals on your journey. Let's see if my musical words and your reflections can uncover some answers to your challenge."

Katy interrupted Buddha Holly, "Don't you need to know what I want on my journey?"

"That is not necessary. We already know," said Buddha Holly, as if he knew all the answers.

Buddha Holly started to prepare himself to address Katy. All the other monks sat down in readiness for his guidance. Katy followed suit.

"If we take wise words, reflect and then transform the meaning into actions, this will give you the answers you seek Katy. Firstly, you must start with the end in mind. This is **visualisation** and means that you must visualise the future that you want. I want you to listen to my words and think, but you cannot interrupt me until I ask you a question. Is that understood?" asked Buddha Holly, looking at Katy.

http://bit.ly/KatyVideo8

"Yes, Buddha Holly," replied Katy, quickly and nervously.

"Now shush Katy, focus on my words now," said Buddha Holly concentrating.

"There is a mountain above us, and I want you to see the top of the mountain as your goal. In your case, that goal is being signed up for the WPFL. Now, you are going to start walking from here to reach the top, and this will represent your journey. Various obstacles and challenges lie ahead, but we must deal with these one by one, and only when they appear."

Buddha Holly collected his thoughts and focused. He then continued Katy's visualisation journey.

"As you start walking up the mountain side, you make good progress and quickly reach a forest. But as you start to go through it, you instantly get lost. You sit down and start to doubt your ability to get to the top, even after just one obstacle. What are you thinking now Katy?" asked Buddha Holly quietly.

"Well, I'm not disappointed, I am just keen to find a way out. So, I am going to try and do just that," said Katy enthusiastically.

Buddha Holly continued the story.

"Something inside you pushes you on and you decide to try and find your way out and within a few minutes you enter the daylight. You have beaten the forest. On the other side is a mountain goat! What does he say to you Katy?" asked Buddha Holly in a serious voice.

"He just says well done?" asked Katy. Before Buddha Holly could reply, Katy started being silly.

"Naaayyyyy" bleated Katy.

"You must be serious Katy," replied Buddha Holly.

"I'm just 'kidding'," said Katy trying to be funnier.

"'Oh Boy', I hope that is the last of your joke fest?" replied Buddha with a smile on his face.

"No, it's not really a joke anymore, I want to be The GOAT….Greatest Of All Time" said Katy.

"You don't hear that 'every day' but I do like it," replied Buddha Holly.

He continued the visualisation.

"He says you did well to get through that forest. Many people have failed just as they have started on their path, but you are different. Let's continue our journey Katy.

"You see your goal ahead and you are making progress towards it, but it still seems a long way off. But every step, no matter how difficult to take, brings you closer. Your journey is getting harder and steeper, but you are developing an inner resilience to carry on. Your determination is rewarded as you come across a gift for you halfway up the mountain. What is that gift and what does it represent Katy?" asked Buddha Holly.

"Is it a drink or some food?" asked Katy.

"It is whatever you say it is Katy," replied Buddha Holly.

"Ok, is it an energy drink that represents a reward for my endeavours so far?" asked Katy.

"There are no wrong answers Katy, only different ones."

"Ok it's a Red Buuuuullllllll!" said Katy as she continued being silly.

"No Katy, less of the animal funny stuff - let's continue.

"You are getting closer to the top of the mountain and your goal is in sight. But now the mountain is steeper, and more challenging. The rocks are slipping beneath your feet and it's colder and scarier. Do you want to stop and go back, even though you are so close Katy?" asked Buddha Holly, challenging Katy.

"No way! I've come this far and I'm not going to give up now!" replied Katy, almost aggressively.

Buddha Holly smiled and continued.

"As you reach the top of the mountain, you reach your goal of playing in the WPFL. Sitting at the very top is a wise old man with your present and the goat. What does he say to you Katy?"

For once, Katy hesitated, unsure of what to say. But she reflected for a moment and then answered Buddha Holly.

"You can do anything you set your mind to Katy, but sometimes this might not be enough?" said Katy questioning her own words.

Buddha Holly saw this puzzled look and it was a look he had been trying to achieve. This was the look of **Self-Realisation**. Buddha Holly started to help Katy work it all out.

"Your journey up the mountain was successful Katy. You took on the forest without doubting yourself. You were rewarded with your gift and this kept you going. Eventually you got to the top and so reached your goal," said Buddha Holly, as he waited for Katy to pick up the thread of the message.

Katy responded with a question.

"So, why might it not be enough?" asked Katy.

"Those were your own words Katy. This may be because there may be other forces at work that may hinder you Katy. Is this self-doubt, is it somebody standing in your way, or is it that you simply realise something that changes your whole approach to your goal?

"It is up to you to work this out as you go through each stage of your life. This is how you visualise success. That is all I can say to you. It is up to you to do your best at these events and reflect as you experience them. When you can do that, then 'that'll be the day' you see success," concluded Buddha Holly who was now humming to himself again.

He then started to sing again, walking off into the distance towards the mountains with the other monks who were also singing behind him. Buddha Holly was happy as he was going to meet Peggy Sue, the first female monk. As they walked into the distance, all that could be heard was the faint sound of the Crickets.

Katy didn't know what to make of her visualisation journey. On the one hand, she had realised she could achieve her goal, but on the other hand, she had to reflect on how to overcome obstacles, maybe even people. But what could these obstacles be? There seemed to be more questions than answers.

Out of the corner of her eye, Katy had noticed something a little odd. Dust clouds were gathering, being whipped up by a lively breeze. The undeniably protective figure of Fred then emerged out of the dust clouds.

"Fred, I think I know why you like this place so much," remarked Katy, looking at Fred.

"Why is that then young Katy?" asked Fred curiously.

"Well, for one, there seems to be a constant gentle breeze and every time I feel a breeze, or even a strong wind, you always appear," said Katy starting to work things out.

"You are learning well Katy," replied Fred.

"Is this a place where you re-charge your mind, rather than your body?" asked Katy.

"That is a *grand* answer Katy, your *mother* would be proud of you. You see Katy, every time I arrive here, I have the same routines which I like to practise. These routines help me to feel grounded and at ease with who I am in life, and a peaceful feeling comes over me, as if I am an Eagle in the sky. These routines also help me to prepare for the challenges that lie ahead on my journey. All I do then is search for an answer to a challenge I am having. I do this by reflecting on my experiences, and by seeking the wise words of the monks. I think we are you now ready for my special **Fred Fix 5 - Tibetan Box Breathing & High 5**" said Fred, as she proceeded to enlighten Katy.

http://bit.ly/KatyVideo9

"Whatever situation you are facing in life, it always helps when we control our breathing. Buddha Holly showed me a **Tibetan Box Breathing** routine which I have adapted. Let me demonstrate this to you now, and then afterwards, tell me if it makes you feel calmer and more focused?" asked Fred, not really expecting a response from Katy.

Katy just nodded and concentrated on Fred and her wise words.

"Imagine a box with four sides. On the first side, just breathe into the count of four seconds and trace the side of the box with your finger. On the second side, hold that breath for four seconds as you trace your finger along its edge. On the third side, breathe out forcibly on each of the four seconds, again as you trace the side with your finger. On the last side, exhale all the remaining breath forcefully, like you are quickly getting all the last bits of air out of your lungs and finish tracing the box. This is Box Breathing. If you do this routine three times it will put you in the '**Zone to Perform**' Katy, then nothing can stop you," said Fred, assertively and knowingly.

Similarly, the **High 5** is a really easy way of becoming calm and it can also help us get in the zone to perform. Hold your hand up and separate your fingers. Then, like tracing the box, just use your index finger of your other hand to trace up your thumb and breath in. As you trace down the thumb you breathe out – do this for each of the remaining four fingers.

Katy had a go at Box Breathing and High 5. She quickly decided that this mental preparation of her mind and body could only be a good thing, especially if Fred and Buddha Holly both used it.

"Once you have got the hang of the Box, we can now add **Mindful Meditation,**" said Fred, knowing that Katy hadn't got a clue what she was talking about.

"You see, being mindful helps us focus on the 'now.' It anchors us clearly in the present moment and gives us clarity. It stops our thoughts running away with themselves, and it is these thoughts that can often lead to poor actions. The trick is to simply focus only on what's happening now and resist all other distracting thoughts of thinking of the past or even the future. Just be in the moment. If a thought comes in, just gently recognise and push it away. This will then pave the way for better performance, and in your case Katy, winning football matches" said Fred.

Fred continued.

"So, follow my instructions, don't get distracted and do exactly as I say," warned Fred. "Now, here are the **5** steps that can be done before you need to perform. This can be done with a fruit like a banana. This is ideal as it's not only getting you in the right frame of mind to perform, but it is also giving you slow release energy which you are going to need if you're performing.

1   Look at the banana. In your head simply describe it to yourself and don't let any other thoughts into your head. If you do get distracted, simply re-focus on the task.
2   Remove the outer skin, hold the banana on your fingers then smell it. Report to yourself what does it feel like, and how does it smell?
3   Break off some of the banana and place it in your mouth and describe the sensation. Report to yourself the sensations, but don't bite or chew it
4   Now chew the banana piece. Report the sensation and taste, but don't swallow the banana piece.
5   Swallow the banana piece and report the sensation.
6   Do this for each part of the remaining parts of the banana.

Katy tried the exercise and with a bit of guidance from Fred eventually remembered the routine.

"So, how was that Katy?" asked Fred keen to know if she liked it.

"It tasted good in the end," said Katy cheekily.

"I know, that's what all children say. But try and practise this and you will find it creates a great platform upon which to perform football skills, especially free kicks and penalties. You know all about them don't you Katy?" said Fred teasing Katy.

"When I put the banana into Mindful Meditation, I call this my **Fred Fix 6 – Banana Boost**," said Fred laughing at her own jokes.

http://bit.ly/KatyVideo10

"Seriously Katy, all I ask is that you try them out, give it a go. What have you got to lose?" said Fred, challenging Katy again.

Fred then answered her own question in a very serious tone of voice.

"You have everything to lose, in football, and in life! Everybody at some point in their life has far too much stress to deal with – it's modern life unfortunately. But we still have to deal with it. Stress builds up, like filling up a bin. If we are not aware of this, and then we don't do anything about it, the bin begins to overflow, with serious consequences for our mental health. We call this our **Stress Bin.**"

http://bit.ly/KatyVideo11

"Is my Stress Bin about to overflow Fred?" asked Katy anxiously.

"No, because now you are aware of it. If you also use my Fred Fixes, these act like an escape valve, releasing your stress. All you need to do is keep practising.

"But remember, there are some stresses we can't control in life, but by just recognising this, you can focus on the stresses you can control. Sometimes, once we have identified a stress, we can even reduce it. For example, you might stress about getting wet in the rain, and you think you can't do anything about it. But then you realise you can use an umbrella to stop yourself getting wet.

"But now Katy, for the final time, let's see what you have learned on your whole amazing journey. Take a *sec* or two to reflect before you answer. The right answer may be far *eastier* than you think.

Here are your final choices and consequences:"

Katy has three **choices** :
1   **Keep reflecting and practising just your favourite ideas and techniques you have learned.**
2   **Keep reflecting and practising all the ideas and techniques you have learned on your whole journey.**
3   **Dismiss all the complicated advice – you always know best.**

Which choice should Katy make?

Here are the **consequences** :

1   This is a good choice. But when things don't go so well, you tend to lose resilience and give up. Your friends can't always rely on you on the pitch. Off the pitch, you carry on with this lack of resilience attitude and get a new nickname of Katy Quitter.
2   You start winning more matches and your team-mates adore you, while the opposition are scared of you. Your football ability keeps improving. The scouts see your ability mindset at school, and whilst recognising you are not the best in every class, you always give 100%. This completes the qualities they are looking for and then rush to sign you up.
3   You thought this was the right choice by believing in yourself and your abilities. A great performer can always adapt and improve within their surroundings. By being unwilling to learn and make changes, you miss this opportunity. This bad habit might show itself at the professional club and the scouts are very reluctant to sign you up.

Katy reflected and thought about all the lessons she had learned on her journey.

"So, Katy, has your reflection altered your choice?" asked Fred wisely.

"I suppose it has Fred. Just taking a little time helps me clear my head," replied a calm Katy.

She decided to pick Choice 2, as she now knew that even though she had her favourite techniques, the other techniques could be useful at different parts of her journey. Fred nodded her approval. But would it really all work out all right in the end?

The mood suddenly changed to a more serious tone. Fred gently put her arm around Katy and asked her to walk towards the helicopter. Katy felt something more important was about to be happen.

In the distance, Katy picked up the noise of the helicopter blades as they started to whirl into action. Surely, it wasn't time to go already. She had only just stepped foot in Tibet! Specs of dust found their way across to her. Within seconds, the dust had turned into a mini tornado, spurred on by the rotating blades.

"Katy, our journey together is almost over. You have learned some important lessons and I am glad I had the chance to help you. But, to bring your goal to reality, you must complete the final part of your journey on your own. Now take your seat in the helicopter and show everyone what the real Katy Cupsworth is all about. I must be somewhere else very soon, but rest assured, I will keep an eye out for you.

"You are going to go far young Katy, like an *Apollo* rocket going to the moon. But in which direction, I am not so sure," said Fred unsure of her destination.

Katy hugged Fred, and reluctantly took her seat in the helicopter. As it rose in the sky, Katy waved and wiped tears away at the same time. As she looked down, Fred was wiping her eyes too. Maybe it was her emotions playing tricks on her, but Fred looked really tired, and so much older.

"Katy are you alright?" shouted Ted and Felicity together.

Katy was sitting on the ground and was dazed – M3 had landed on her hard, albeit 'accidentally.'

Ted and Felicity raced on to the pitch to help Katy.

"What's your name?" asked Felicity trying to establish if Katy had concussion.

"Fred?" replied Katy drowsily.

"Wow, Katy really is concussed, she thinks her name is Fred," said Felicity anxiously.

Ted interrupted.

"Tell her she is Marta and maybe she might get us the equaliser," said Ted trying to make a joke out of the situation.

"Ted stop it now….and take those knickers off Katy's head!" demanded Felicity.

Katy recognised mum and dad, but it was as if she couldn't speak to them, and they couldn't hear her if she did….like a fuzzy dream.

Slowly Katy came to, and everything came back to being normal again. "I'm fine, but where am I?"

"You're on Belmont Rec playing Frenchwood. M3 just sat on you. Are you ok? Where does it hurt? Do you want to carry on?" asked Felicity firing question after question at her confused daughter.

"I think I'm ok, but where is Fred?" asked Katy looking at Felicity.

"Oh Katy, what are you saying? I think that accidental bump to your head has given you concussion," said Felicity, as Ted waved three fingers at Katy and asked her how many he was holding up.

Katy's mind was in over-drive.

"We qualified for the IT by not getting any red cards against Anchor Inn WFC. I know we eventually lost the IT, but did we win the League and Cup double?" asked Katy trying to piece everything together.

"Steady on Katy, there is no team called Anchor Inn WFC and we still need to qualify for the IT. As for the double, even a team with eleven Katy Cupsworths can't win that as we have yet to play most of our matches!" said Ted guessing that Katy was worse than she looked.

"But I missed a penalty in Holland, and we lost and…" before she could finish the sentence, Felicity interrupted to save her embarrassment.

"Katy, the IT is held over Christmas, and it's only October?" she said trying to reason with Katy.

Katy started to reflect. Did she really meet Fred and go on an amazing journey? Or was it the 'accidental' bump from Frenchwood Park's M3 that had given her weird thoughts which had been brought on by concussion?

Katy didn't know why, but she took some deep breaths and reflected on her current plight. Then she had a clear thought. No matter what she thought had happened on her journey with Fred, she somehow felt different, better in many ways. Now though wasn't the time to reflect anymore, that could wait. Now was the time to get up and start showing Frenchwood Park how good a team Belmont Avenue were. This was the time to put all her Fred learning into practice!

"Dad, it's three fingers, and mum I was just teasing about Holland and the IT. We talked about Holland in a Geography lesson last week," said Katy quickly getting her mind into gear.

"Ok, ref, she's ok….no sub this time, can we get on with it," said Ted urging the ref to re-start the game.

Ranvir passed the ball quickly to Katy who instantly started to race towards the goal.

There was a problem though. Ahead of her was the imposing figure of M3 who was stood waiting for her on the D of the penalty area, like a spider waiting to catch a fly!

As Katy looked up at M3 she thought she had double vision. Was M3 stood on two D's or was this what the voice had said…. was Doubting Debbie trying to put her off? Katy shook her head to clear her vision.

It was then that she remembered the advice from Fred which told her to ignore Doubting Debbie and not be scared of M3. Katy spontaneously shouted out, "One on one big girl, now it's my turn to show you who's the mummy!" It was if she was talking to both M3 and Doubting Debbie.

M3 was fuming. "Who do you think you are Katy Cupsworth?" raged M3, as she threw her body at Katy, trying to show her who was in charge on the pitch.

As M3 lunged at her, Katy had belief in herself. She was not going to be put off this time. With a twist of her hips, and a deft flick of the ball, and without breaking her stride, Katy evaded the lunge of M3. Now it was M3's turn to be sprawled out in the mud. Katy dribbled the ball towards the goals, before sliding it past the keeper. She was the match winner.

The joyous Belmont Avenue team lifted Katy on their shoulders and took her off the pitch in style.

"Mr Cupsworth, can I have a word please?" said a woman in the power suit who was now walking on to the pitch to approach Ted.

"I'm Lady Sugar, the Chairperson of the WPFL. We are holding some global trials in Chicago, USA at the end of the month. We want to improve the quality of players in our new league and would like to attract players from all over the world. Would you allow us to take Katy with us for this major showcase trial?"

Unable to speak, Ted looked at Felicity. They both nodded together. They knew how much this meant to Katy, and although Felicity had some reservations about missing school, it really was too good an opportunity to miss.

"Yes, that would be fine Lady Sugar!" replied Ted and Felicity together.

"That's great.... you're hired!" said Lady Sugar emphatically.

Mission 6 Questions

- What is the "Monk's Temple"?
- Describe visualisation.
- What does GOAT stand for and who is your GOAT?
- Describe the Fred Fix – Tibetan Box Breathing.
- Describe the Fred Fix – Mindful Meditation.
- Describe the Fred Fix – Banana Boost.
- Why is knowing about a "stress bin" important?

Key Words

Monk's Temple	Zone to Perform
Visualisation	Mindful Meditation
Self-Realisation	Fred Fix 6 Banana Boost
Fred Fix 5 Tibet Box Breathing & High 5	

Global Video Mission 6:

http://bit.ly/KatyCupH

Conclusion

I'M NOT A PRO FOOTBALLER YET... GET ME IN HERE!!

Concussion or not, Katy is ready for the trial
But will her new-found skills make the scouts smile
Will she get signed up and get loads of fans
Or will she say no thanks, as she has other plans.

I n the few weeks leading up to the trials, Katy could hardly forget about Fred and still believed in her, yet maybe it really was a result of her knock on the head, and her amazing journey didn't really happen after all?

However, she put all thoughts of Fred, and her lessons learned, to the back of her mind and focused on her football skills. She also felt a need to apply herself in school. It was as if something had changed within Katy. This aspect of Katy's development did not go unnoticed by her teachers, and her parents. She was demonstrating more belief in herself, she was developing her resilience and not giving up so quickly at subjects she didn't like or found hard. She was empathetic to the teacher's needs and all this led to her developing her ability mindset. Finally, her mindful mental state brought out all the best in her learning.

Slowly, but surely, the date for the trials in Chicago arrived. Each triallist from England was accompanied by parents or relatives and they all arrived a couple of days before the trials so that they could recover from jet lag. It did seem a long way to go for just one game of football, but this one game could make or break the dreams of each and every player.

Chicago was a massive city, with many millions of people. The football arena was in an exclusive downtown area and the crowds quickly built up in anticipation of seeing new talent from around the world. This in itself made most of the players a little in awe, and even scared the coaches and parents. The scene was set to discover who was good enough to progress on their journey and get signed up by the WPFL.

A familiar figure addressed the crowds ahead of the big kick off. It was no other than the ex-FIFA President who was eventually ousted from office after a long drawn-out affair. It was Stepdown Later, and as was his nature, he was still clinging to power.

"Welcome to the WPFL Global Trials. We anticipated a big crowd, but my oh my, nothing as big as what I am now witnessing. We are indeed fortunate to be hosting this event as we will see some of the brightest football talent in the world, and in what better place to host it than Chicago, the Windy City. This is a fabulous opportunity for players to make a name for themselves," said Stepdown, thinking he too could make a bit of money.

The crowd cheered, and the referee blew her whistle to signal teams to prepare for the match. Katy couldn't help but think that something special was about to happen. 'Windy City', surely that had to be a good omen for Fred to come along and help out?

The match was being played between two representative sides. It would be UK & Europe versus the Rest of the World. As the UK & Europe team was announced Katy felt a sudden surge of panic. Included in her team were no other than Evie 'Evil' Hazard, Dee Dee 'Ego' Eggers and the infamous Sanchez Sisters. Fred must have been real after all she thought.

Katy was now becoming more than a little confused and anxious, and the match hadn't even kicked off yet. In the distance, Katy was then distracted by something else. A group of girls had begun skipping 'Double Dutch' style and a woman was waving at her from the touchline…was this Doubting Debbie again?

The referee blew her whistle for UK & Europe to kick off and the ball quickly found Katy on the left wing.

"Pass the ball Cupsworth, I'm free" shouted Sarina Sanchez.

Katy was in a trance like state, and an opposition player quickly nicked the ball from her possession.

"She's rubbish," shouted Sadia as she chased back to trip up the opposition player, giving away a needless free kick.

This wasn't the start Katy was expecting.

Whether it was coincidence or not, the famous Chicago wind started to blow. Katy remembered this as a sign that Fred was nearby and waited for some much-needed intervention.

Whatever help Katy thought she needed didn't arrive. She was on her own to deal with her thoughts, and the consequences of her actions.

"Ref, I'm hurt!" shouted Katy.

The ref blew her whistle.

"Ok, time out ladies. Trainer can you sort out this young girl?" asked the ref politely, but with a little impatience as the match had barely started and already she was injured.

Katy though wasn't injured. The introduction of the trainer gave Katy an opportunity to collect her thoughts and reflect. It would have been easy to react to the situation of confusion and panic by either giving up or getting angry. Yet, Katy had quickly reflected on a response, a green response. Whether Fred was real or not, she wasn't coming to help out now. It was clearly up to her to resolve the situation. Maybe this was an opportunity to banish Doubting Debbie once and for all?

After a few quick box breaths, Katy was filled with a new-found sense of purpose and commitment. Gone were the last traces of Doubting Debbie. In her place was a visualisation of future success and an unshakeable belief that she now had everything she needed to achieve success. Katy got to her feet ready to resume play.

Frustrated by this stoppage, the Sanchez Sisters went into over-drive and each got a yellow card for over enthusiastic tackling! Dee Dee then decided she wanted to be the solo star and took a long shot at goal, when a simple pass would have kept possession and gained a better shooting opportunity. This made Evie mad and she lost concentration. The whole team was cracking up and Katy could see what was happening.

Suddenly another gust of wind blew across the pitch and lifted the ball out over the nearby fence. Katy realised this timely intervention was a sign from Fred, and took the opportunity to have an impromptu motivational 'pep talk.' Katy spoke slowly and clearly. She talked about how much skill they had, and why sneakily injuring players, getting frustrated and being distracted, was stopping them from showcasing their great talents. The team instantly got the message.

After the re-start, things seemed different. The team was more focused and had moved up a gear. Katy found herself wide open in the opposition penalty area and shouted for the ball. Dee Dee for once didn't try to show off by dribbling through all the players, but instead picked out Katy with an exquisite pass. Katy feinted to shoot, and instead laid the ball off to Evie Hazard, who returned the ball back to Katy. All that was left was for Katy to unleash her 'Screamer' which she duly did. One – nil.

The crowd went wild, along with the scouts and the UK & Europe parents. They had just witnessed a shot so powerful and accurate, that even two goalkeepers could not stop it. As play re-started, the UK & Europe team started to play as a real team. There seemed to be team empathy, an understanding, that wasn't there before. As a team, they supported each other, and nobody was hogging the spotlight by trying to be a superstar. Katy was leading from the front by encouraging all her teammates. Soon Katy's team scored a second goal, and then a third. Katy was happy to be a team player, assisting others whenever she could. Soon the match as a contest was over, with UK & Europe team eventually running out 4-0 winners.

As Katy came off the pitch, she was approached by an important person.

"I am Ivor Contract. The Katy Cupsworth I saw today wasn't the same Katy Cupsworth I saw a few months ago back in England. You have changed! Whatever you have done and whoever you have worked with to create this change, well, the results have been phenomenal," said Mr Contract.

Then Mr Contract strangely said his name again to Katy.

"I know, you're Ivor Contract," replied Katy slightly bemused.

"No, I've a contract…. for you Katy! We want to offer you a contract for one of our nurture teams in the WPFL!" exclaimed Ivor excitedly.

Katy couldn't respond. This was all she had ever wanted. She dashed off to find her mum and dad and tell them the exciting news.

"We're over here Katy!" screamed Felicity, as Ted rushed towards Katy and enveloped her in a big hug.

"What a great game Katy! On and off the ball you were amazing. We're so proud of you!" exclaimed Ted as Felicity smiled.

"Mum, dad, I have some good news for you," said Katy. "I have a contract to play in the WPFL" she added with a touch of sadness in her voice. "But you know what, I'm going to say no!" said Katy putting on a brave face.

"Katy, why?" asked a startled Ted.

"Don't get me wrong, I am happy to have been chosen, but I think I need to focus more on my own abilities outside football now. I need to develop myself as a whole person especially in school before I think about joining the WPFL. So, I am going to tell Mr Contract to ask me again in a couple of years…as long as that's ok with you guys?" asked Katy looking at her mum and dad.

Mum and Dad nodded their agreement.

"That's really good news Katy, a sensible decision," said Felicity looking across at Ted anxiously.

"Well, we have some news for you too Katy," said Ted with more than a touch of sadness in his own voice.

Ted took hold of Katy and looked her in the eye before telling her their news.

"Katy, we didn't want to tell you before your trial, as we didn't want to put you off. But yesterday we received a telephone call from England. Sadly, Grandma Wyn passed away last night, just a few days away from her 88th birthday."

Katy was shocked and a little stunned. Tears started to form in her eyes as the sad news took hold of Katy's emotions. Katy hugged her mum and dad in silence and reflected on the news.

A minute or so passed before Ted took the opportunity to say something else.

"Grandma Wyn had a wonderful life helping others. She created a beautiful legacy of love and support for her family and friends."

Felicity continued Ted's sentiments.

"But she was getting tired and I suspect she was missing Grandad Bob, and your cousin Danni. She has her own family again now and I'm sure she will always be with you in spirit"

Katy produced a little forced smile that was tinged with sadness.

"I will never forget her mum. I do hope her spirit never leaves me," replied Katy.

"Never Katy," replied Felicity.

Ted interrupted.

"This might not be the best time to tell you this Katy, but your mum and I have some other news for you," said Ted looking strangely anxious and excited at the same time.

"A long time ago, before you were born, I fell in love with a beautiful woman while I was coaching over the summer here in Chicago. This woman was on holiday with her family and was only 18 at the time. To cut a long story short, we married a few years later. But sadly, somewhere along the way I lost sight of who I was and how remarkable she was, and we separated."

"But Dad, why didn't you tell us that? What about mum? When did you meet her?" asked Katy in utter disbelief and confusion.

"Hang on Katy. The woman I met in Chicago was your beautiful mother! I lost track of us and focused all my energies on getting you into the WPFL. This pushed us apart and your mum recognised that you needed a more balanced upbringing, hence why we split up," said Ted, looking fondly across at Felicity.

Katy looked at her mum and dad with a relief that was almost tangible. Felicity continued where Ted had left off.

"So, our news is that we are going to re-marry in Chicago before we fly home!" said Felicity who was now about to burst into tears of happiness.

"That really is great news, and are we going to live as a real family again when we get back?" asked Katy.

"Of course, Katy, but this time I will listen to your mum about what's best for you," said Ted.

It had been a bittersweet experience in Chicago, and it was a trip the whole Cupsworth family would never forget.

Back in England, life carried on with Ted and Felicity growing stronger together day by day. Katy was making good progress at school, and was really enjoying her football, without the pressure of trying to join the WPFL. Everything was going well as a family, but Katy still had something she needed to do – visit the cemetery to say goodbye to Grandma Wyn.

It was a still summer's day as Katy carried some flowers to the grave. Katy was in a reflective mood as she laid the flowers down at her headstone, next to a lone plastic mini windmill which had been left by one of Grandma Wyn's family.

Katy looked at the headstone of Grandma Wyn and spoke out loud.

"Grandma Wyn, I do miss you. I know you had to leave us to look after Grandad Bob and Danni. But I will always try and make you proud," said Katy holding back her tears.

As Katy turned away from the grave, she noticed that the little arms of the windmill were turning faster and faster, yet there was no wind to propel them. Then something stranger happened.

"Katy, I knew I would see you again!"

Katy couldn't see anyone, but the voice was instantly recognisable. It was Fred.

"Fred, what are you doing here?" asked Katy still in shock.

"Haven't you worked it all out yet, dear Katy?" asked Fred.

Katy shook her head slowly with a puzzled look on her face.

"Well, let me go through some clues for you Katy. Remember when I said what **type** of person are you in Mission 1 on Frenchwood Rec? This was a reference to my typing exploits at the factory. In Mission 2 in Delft, I said you must **work it out**. That was a clue to my background owning and running a gym. I also threw in the **Windmills** too as this was a dead giveaway to my name.

"In Mission 3, I said try and **exercise** your brain and don't get **hot headed**. Again, I was telling you about the gym and the sauna. In Mission 4 I mentioned my **learning journeys** which was a reference to my travels when I was younger. I also said don't get **caught-cold** thinking about it too much. This was another reference to my factory work at Courtaulds. In Mission 5, I even **wincked** at you which was a reference to my education at Winckley Square. Do you need me to explain the remaining clues?"

Katy was in shock and could barely speak. Fred continued.

"Remember, I said it's not a **Con**, and you must not **vent** your anger on me. This was about my days learning at the **Convent**.

"Finally, in Mission 6, I mentioned that is a '**grand**' answer Katy, your '**mother**' would be proud of you. Then I said take a **sec** or two to reflect before you answer. The right answer is **far eastier** than you think. This was a reference to my job as a secretary and my learning journeys in the Far East. My best clue though was the last clue when I mentioned travelling to the moon in the **Apollo** rocket – this was a reference to our Apollo gym.

"So, I am a little disappointed that you couldn't work it all out. It was me, your Grandma Wyn or Winifred as some people called me. I liked the sound of Fred, so I used that name to speak to you!" said Fred getting caught up in all the excitement of revealing her identity.

"But this is not all about me. It's all about you Katy. How you learned on your amazing journey, how you learned new skills and new ways of thinking. Ultimately, you changed and improved your game, but you also realised football was only a part of your journey. In fact, your journey was a story of two halves so to speak. In the first half of your journey you were desperate to join the WPFL, but in the second half you realised your football ambitions were maybe not as crucial as you once thought. That is true learning and progress Katy, and I couldn't be prouder of you.

"I don't know whether you knew this or not, but your 'Screamer' of a shot was also a great way for me to keep track of your progress in your key areas of development - **S**elf-esteem, **C**onfidence, **R**esilience, **E**mpathy, **A**bility, and **M**indful mental health. So always remember Katy, if in doubt, just **SCREAM**.

"You don't need me so much now, as you're firmly on your path to being a success at whatever you decide to do, football or something else. But if it's ever windy, or you see a windmill, always think of me and my spirit will always guide you," said Fred waving goodbye.

Katy called out one last time.

"But what shall I call you now…Wyn, Winifred or Fred?" asked Katy.

Fred replied, "I don't care, any really, except never call me Winnie. I always hated being called Winnie and I am not going to change now!"

On her way home, Katy bumped into her cousin Chris.

"Chris, I believe your amazing journey now. I have just been on one!" said Katy excitedly.

"Did you meet Grandad Bob…. Alf, I mean?" asked Chris eagerly.

"No, I met Fred…. Winifred…I mean Grandma Wyn, and she was amazing," said Katy unable to conceal her secret any longer.

Chris smiled.

"They were great people weren't they Katy? And we have been so lucky to see them again and learn from them," said Chris, with a touch of sadness in his voice.

Katy nodded in agreement. They both knew that what they had learned must now be put into practice otherwise they would be letting down their grandparents. Chris and Katy made a pact to continue their journeys and help each other, in memory of Grandad Bob and Grandma Wyn.

Katy's mood was uplifted. She said goodbye to Chris and raced home to tell her mum about what had happened at Grandma Wyn's grave.

"Mum, mum, you will never guess what happened to me when I visited Grandma Wyn's grave today..." but then Katy stopped. Her mum would never believe her, and more to the point, she might think Katy was making it up, a bit like she thought her cousin Chris did with his amazing journey.

Instead, Katy whisked herself off to bed. It had been a very tiring day and her head was still a little confused and she didn't feel like thinking too much.

Felicity followed Katy upstairs to her bedroom, worried.

"It's ok Mum, I do miss Grandma Wyn you know, but I know she is always with me in spirit."

Felicity smiled. "I know she is," she said, as she folded Katy's discarded clothes and smoothed down the covers.

"Now, young lady, it's time for Fred."

"What...time for Fred?" said Katy, looking at her mother wide-eyed. "Do you know about Fred?"

"Oh, er, bed!" said Felicity, quickly. "I meant time for bed. What else did you think I meant? You have been spending far too much time with your cousin Chris!

Goodnight Katy darling!"

Conclusion

- When Katy recovered from the bump on her head, what did she realise about her journey?
- List the three crucial clues that have been given about Fred's identity.
- Did you suspect who Fred was before finding out it was Grandma Wyn?
- List six things you have learned from your journey with Katy.

If you want to challenge yourself further, visit:

You can locate all the Katy videos here:

Scream 48

Why not measure your **SCREAM 48** score again and compare your scores from the start of the book? Answer each question with only one answer. Add up your scores after 12 questions to find your **SCREAM 48.**

1   You value yourself highly in terms of your own achievements and qualities
     Strongly Agree – Agree – Disagree – Strongly Disagree

2   You doubt your self-worth in terms of your own abilities
     Strongly Agree – Agree – Disagree – Strongly Disagree

3   You are rarely scared of life's day to day challenges
     Strongly Agree – Agree – Disagree – Strongly Disagree

4   If you feel nervous, these feelings can often stop you attempting challenges
     Strongly Agree – Agree – Disagree – Strongly Disagree

5   You can often give up completing challenges
     Strongly Agree – Agree – Disagree – Strongly Disagree

6   You recognise the need to re-charge and review your strengths if you can't complete a challenge
     Strongly Agree – Agree – Disagree – Strongly Disagree

7   More often than not, you consider the needs of others
     Strongly Agree – Agree – Disagree – Strongly Disagree

8   You will agree to a group decision even if you feel you're in the right
     Strongly Agree – Agree – Disagree – Strongly Disagree

9   You feel you have certain strengths and certain weaknesses
     Strongly Agree – Agree – Disagree – Strongly Disagree

10   You think over time you can't improve your strengths and can't reduce
     your weaknesses
     Strongly Agree – Agree – Disagree – Strongly Disagree

11   You are calm in a stressful situation
     Strongly Agree – Agree – Disagree – Strongly Disagree

12   You don't have a range of skills and strategies which allow you to
     overcome nerves
     Strongly Agree – Agree – Disagree – Strongly Disagree

Scores:

	Strongly Agree	Agree	Disagree	Strongly Disagree
1	4	3	2	1
2	1	2	3	4
3	4	3	2	1
4	1	2	3	4
5	1	2	3	4
6	4	3	2	1
7	4	3	2	1
8	4	3	2	1
9	4	3	2	1
10	1	2	3	4
11	4	3	2	1
12	1	2	3	4

Results:

1-12   You are at the beginning of your journey. With good support and your sustained efforts, you may well make progress and go far on your journey to a better you.

13-24   You have made some progress, but you need to keep going. Learn from your mistakes and be prepared to keep pushing yourself and your journey may well surprise you.

25-36   You have made good progress and there is more to come if you continue to learn and apply yourself.

37-48   You have made excellent progress, but you can get complacent. You must keep learning, help others, and see the value in your journey.

Keywords

in the order they appear in the book

Fear of Failure Being scared to try because you fear getting things wrong.

Role Model Someone you look up to and try to be like.

Self-Esteem How much we believe in our self.

Physical Self-Worth How much we accept, value and celebrate our appearance.

Fred Fix A special way to improve.

Confidence Not being scared to think, say, or act.

Smarter Confidence Knowing the difference between being confident and over-confident or arrogant.

Fred Fix 1 – Balloon Blow A way to collect all our qualities and achievements to remind us of all the progress we are making.

Fred Fix 1 – Balloon Pop A way to collect all our barriers to success, and then pop them.

Resilience To keep going, or to retreat and re-charge before trying again. Having compassion for ourselves.

Fail Forward Learning from our mistakes so next time we have a better chance of success.

Fail Backward Not learning from our mistakes, and maybe making the same mistakes over and over again.

Achilles Heel   Our one major weakness.

Red React or   React is often quick and not thought out and can result in poor
Green Respond   outcomes. Respond means to think about an appropriate response
before acting and this generally results in better outcomes.

'Reflect'   This is when we think about how to get success if we don't succeed
Resilience   at first.
(a potato &
a straw)

Fred Fix 2 –   A way to re-focus ourselves in readiness for a challenge by flicking an
Elastic Band Flick   elastic band against our wrist.

Team Empathy   Understanding the needs of others, understanding each other's
strengths and weaknesses and supporting each other.

Leader Empathy   Understanding the needs of individuals within a team, and having
the confidence to tell people where they are going wrong, or right.

Constructive   Challenging words that are said that may not be liked, or wanted,
Criticism   but are needed. They are intended to help individuals improve,
to give help to someone without any personal bias or fear ie to
genuinely help them improve.

Fred Fix 3 –   A way to help others by giving good feedback, followed by
Eat The Burger   challenging constructive feedback, followed by good positive feedback.

Ability Mindset   Believing you can do something by effort, practice, guidance
Skills   and resilience.

Success-Not-Yet   When you don't succeed at something, but you don't give up in
readiness for success next time. It is success, but not quite yet.

Fred Fix 4 – Amy Buster	Breathing in and think about Amy being upset. Then breathe out and see Amy smiling.
Fred Fix 4 – Star Trek Fingers	A simple way to control our emotions through breathing in, making a positive image and squeezing the finger and thumb together to anchor a great thought in readiness for action.
Monk's Temple	An exercise to recognise negative thoughts, but then allow them to leave you.
Visualisation	To see your future you must start with the end in mind ie identify and see what you want. This helps us believe we can achieve our future goals.
Self-Realisation	When you eventually realise what you need to do to get success.
Fred Fix 5 – Tibetan Box Breathing	A simple way to control our emotions by drawing a box in the air. Side 1 breathing in, Side 2 holding the breath, Side 3 breathing out and then Side 4 quickly breathing out the remaining air.
High Five	Using the open palm of one hand, trace the thumb up and breathe in. As you descend the thumb, breathe out. Do this for the other four fingers. Try and let no thoughts come into your mind.
Zone to Perform	Clearing your mind in readiness for action.
Fred Fix 6 – Mindful Meditation	A way to focus just on the 'now' and not get distracted by other thoughts, positive or negative.
Fred Fix 7 – Banana Boost	A combination of Tibetan Box Breathing and Mindful Meditation where a sequence of instructions is completed in readiness for performance.

Stress Bin   Where we collect and identify our stresses, both those we can control and those we can't. This may also be a place where you can actually reduce your stresses by reflecting and using the coping mechanisms you have learned.

SCREAM   **S**elf-Worth, **C**onfidence, **R**esilience, **E**mpathy, **A**bility, & **M**indful mental health.

Contact Details:

Ross McWilliam
BA Hons, MSc, PGCE, LCSP, CMI Level 7
Mental Health First Aid England Accredited (MHFA)

Tel   07771 916788
E   ross@rossmcwilliam.com
E   info@mindsetpro.co.uk
W   www.katyjourney.com
W   www.mindsetpro.co.uk